Hello

Everyone Has a Story

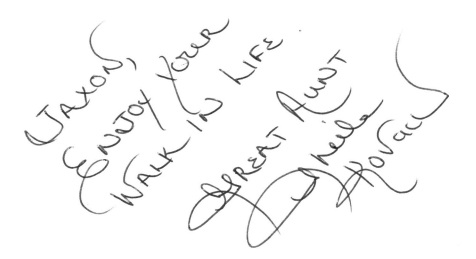

Jaxon,
Enjoy Your
Walk In Life

Great Aunt
Sheila
Kovach

SHEILA KOVACH

ISBN 978-1-64191-332-4 (paperback)
ISBN 978-1-64191-333-1 (digital)

Christian Faith Publishing, Inc.
832 Park Avenue
Meadville, PA 16335
www.christianfaithpublishing.com

Printed in the United States of America

I would like to dedicate this book to my husband, Jere, for his constant support, encouragement, and love. As we have walked through this world together, he has been my best friend and companion. My prayer is that I can keep him twitterpated for the rest of our lives.

Contents

Hello and the Stories behind the Responses

WALKING HAS ALWAYS BEEN A favorite pastime of mine. I enjoy the sights and sounds of the outdoors. God created so many beautiful environments for us to enjoy, we just need to get out and open our eyes and enjoy our time in the outdoors.

I love to observe people and have always wondered, "What's their story?" Our life history and current condition is a private hidden thing until we choose to reveal it. To the everyday-path walking person, we reveal nothing verbally as we pass by. However, the manner in which a person responds or does not respond to a hello is quite telling. Watching a person's mannerisms, eye contact, and general facial expressions tells a passerby a lot.

During my daily walks, I have gathered a lot of thoughts about my fellow walkers. This is a book of fiction. Some stories are made up of a little truth, but details are altered to create a book of fiction. My prayer is that we all can see a little of ourselves and have a little understanding of what possibly might be the fellow walker's life, as we read through this tale of walking and just simply saying hello.

Preface

WINTERS ARE LONG AND VERY cold in Northern Dakota. I can very well see why the Scandinavians settled here to farm and conduct business. For all the beauty of the spring, summer, and fall, winters are brutal.

After retiring, I found that I needed to keep my body moving for a few hours a day or I would never be able to wear my current wardrobe. As much as I enjoy walking, it now became more of a health incentive than something to do just for enjoyment. From everything I have read in the AARP (American Association of Retired Persons) bulletin, walking is one of the best things a person my age can do.

I came from a small Wyoming town and live now in a rural Wyoming area. Roads are not all paved in this neck of the woods, and depending on where you want to walk, you walk on dirt and rocks. I do enjoy the walking trails, and the few that are paved are a delight to me. I was very happy to discover the paved walking paths in this northern town and eagerly got out and checked them out with a nice walk. I timed my walks in different directions and distances so I could choose a path that fit my time limit that particular day. If I had an hour, two hours, or three hours, I could be home within the time period. Imagine my joy when I discovered a park with paved walking paths and a beautifully maintained park experience for all to enjoy.

I very much love it and, after four years, have some tales to tell from what I have experienced.

This is my story.

Hello.

Shakey Business

TODAY I WALK WITH THE park waking to spring. Almost all the cold winter snow and ice is gone. New growth has started on the grounds, and the trees are just ready to burst with an abundance of new leaves and growth.

The geese are returning from wintering elsewhere and are setting up domestication. Some ganders are already standing guard as their goose of choice is sitting on a clutch of eggs. Several sets of younger geese are still playing the mating game and fill the air with their honks and verbal conversations.

There are only a few walkers out as most do not like the cooler air. I find the lower temperatures very enjoyable as I have a lower tolerance for getting too hot. Each completed loop on the path takes me exactly one-half hour. I find it interesting how many things can change in a half hour; such is the case so very often.

Today I approached a woman about my age who stooped forward to walk in a hurry. I say hello as we pass, and she only nods. I wonder at her hurry-up nature, not knowing that she doesn't dare leave her retired husband at home for very long by himself. She doesn't trust him to handle things by himself for any length of time. Thank God for *The Price Is Right* as she knows that for at least one hour he will be occupied while she quickly makes two laps on the trail.

They had had a good life, raised a family of two boys and two girls. He had been a carpenter and a craftsman of fine cabinetry.

Because he got his skills from an old-world craftsman, his work was highly sought-after. Many new built homes were fortunate to have the beautiful cabinetry he was famous for. When he was a young man in training, the old-world master would patiently work with the young man. His key advice was to not hurry. "Take your time and treat the wood as if she were a lady." He wouldn't understand that sentiment until he worked many years in the shop. Now he understood that treating the wood with gentleness and taking his time produced the best results.

He started noticing the shaking in his hands in his forties. It had come on gradually. When it first started, it was almost funny. They would have to clean up the few slops of coffee or whatever missed his mouth, but now it was a nightmare. He isn't able to hang on to anything, and the messes he makes are hourly. His wife finds no joy in cleaning up the constant messes.

Along with the shaking came the anger and unhappiness. Not able to continue with his craft, he was very frustrated. So was his wife.

All their married life, he was the strong one, taking care of everything. She trusted that that would be the case always. She doesn't know at what point she got mad, she just did. Now she is mad a lot. She's mad at their aging bodies, their kids who never stop by, the cold weather, God for letting this happen, and her husband. She feels guilty for blaming him, it's a disease after all, but she feels let down. This isn't what she had planned. It just isn't fair.

Someone told her a long time ago that the secret to everything is age. She wonders why it's a secret, because a person really should be warned—to prepare for it and to learn how to deal with the age-related issues.

I pass her one more time, and she recognizes me from the first pass. I get another half smile and a nod. Little do I know that as she arrives home, he has finished his show and is now burning toast in the toaster, and there is spilled coffee all over the kitchen floor.

2

Pastoral Walk

TODAY IS ANOTHER NICE SPRING day but a little breezy. The huge old oaks sing with the wind. I wonder how old they are and who planted them. A few branches tired of hanging on to old weathered trunks came down with the gusts that blew all night. They are easy to step around, and the park employees will clear them to the side when they do the path drive through.

I like the wind; it cleans the stagnation and puts new oxygen into my lungs. There comes a point when it's too strong, but today it is very nice.

The river around the park is not unfrozen yet, and the wind has blown loose garbage and trash onto the ice. It looks bad, and that is one thing about the wind that is on its negative list.

I pass a gentleman with coat and scarf who says good morning when I say hello. He's in no hurry, just ambling along, enjoying the sights.

He has come to the park for thirty years. Today, as like the last five years, he comes alone. His daughter came with him a few times four-and-a-half years ago, but cannot now that she got her teaching job. He is so proud of her as she became a teacher like her mother. It's a gift to work with other people's children. So many cannot be kind and patient with children who are not raised the way they would raise a child. He was lucky to have one child, and she has always been daddy's little girl, even now at thirty-six years old. He remembers how he and his wife planned for their child. She was born in the summer so her mother could spend the newness of having her first child with her every day. She took the first-time-mother experience pretty seriously. Man, she was a hoverer. He remembers feeling that he was one clumsy, inexperienced man, as he did everything wrong. That little girl would not stay wrapped up in her blanket in his arms, and he could never burp her right. Funny how motherhood just came naturally to his wife. She was radiant with their little red-haired bundle of love.

The child kept both of them enthralled with how smart she was and how cute she looked in everything his wife put her in. He thinks of the photos of her on her first day of school and the ones with her flute in hand. He recalls her with her fluffy black dog playing catch with a stick in the yard. His wife and daughter did most everything together. He beamed with pride as the two of them made cookies and pies. He enjoyed the fashion shows as his daughter modeled the latest skirt or dress his wife sewed for her. He was tickled that his daughter followed in her mother's footsteps and took to sewing, cooking, cleaning, teaching, and matters of her faith, just like her mom. He doesn't remember a time that they didn't get along.

They had no problems with his daughter during her teenage years. She ran around with girls from quality families, and there was a lot of activity at his home as all the girls loved to gather there as they had plenty of room and there were no brothers or sisters to bug them.

His wife had a way with children, adolescents and preteens. She was a favorite teacher to most every child she had in her class. She made each child feel special and gave undivided attention to the children who very much felt left out, alone, or insecure. She was a blessing to many children over her teaching career.

God, he missed her. His wife was a kind, soft-spoken, happy woman. It just didn't seem fair that she got breast cancer. She hated her breasts. She never showed them off, wore revealing clothes, or drew any attention to them at all. Unlike a lot of women and young girls, his wife had class. She was a soft, classy woman. He loved her from the time he saw her first eating lunch with friends at the summer Christian church camp. He went every year as his father was the pastor. She came with friends. At fourteen, she had no plans to do anything else that summer, so there she was. At the evening vespers, he was introduced to her, and they hit it off immediately.

As he walks, he remembers their youth and young-adult lives. This then began the beginning of a lifelong friendship and love. Walking hand in hand with her through this life was a happiness that they both cherished. The final year of the cancer is too hard on his emotions to dwell on. He suffered her loss long before she left this world. He whispers to God to take care of his sweet love until he can join her.

I did not see him on my second lap and know that it is quite common for walkers only to take one lap. As years went by, I realized that he only walked on Mondays. As with his daughter following in his wife's footsteps, he also followed in his father's footsteps. Monday was his day off, so to speak, as his pastoral duties kept him busy the other six days a week.

Difficult Roads

TODAY, AS I WALK, I am again so happy to see Mother Nature in youthful spring. Snow drifts melting to expose new growth and the earth renewing itself. What was a difficult winter could well be turning into a very nice spring.

A very elderly couple approaches me, and I can tell that they are new to this walking trail, as they comment on each and everything they approach. They both say hello to my hello, but he says, "Hello, young lady." This makes me laugh as I am a grandma and been married for way over half my life. I say to have a lovely day, and they respond that they will.

They are strolling today in the park as they had come to visit their daughter and her family who had moved to this city so she could work in health care for a nursing home. They had not ever been to this state or city and had been encouraged to go check out the park. As they strolled, something in the quieter sound the geese made reminded her of a very long time ago when she was a child. It made her think of lying in bed and hearing the soft cries of her mother as she wept on the other side of the bedroom wall. She remembered that soft whimpering most every night during most of her childhood. She knew it had something to do with her father leaving. He had just left. One day he was there, then he was gone forever. She never saw him again. She never fully heard the story of why he left or what the details were until she was a young woman and was getting ready to leave home as she was to be married.

Her mother took full responsibility to raise her and her sister and brother. She was the oldest and had responsibilities to do too. Her brother was a sickly baby, and while her mother took in laundry to make money to support the family, she held her brother. Her mom believed that if her son were to die, then he would not die without knowing he was loved. So he slept in her arms, and then when her mother could take him, she carried and held him every second she could possibly spare. He was always with physical touch from her, her mother, her aunts, grandparents, her sister, and a few kind friends. He was in no way spoiled; he was fragile, and he was shown much love.

As the years went by, she watched her mother's determination to provide for the family. She had a variety of jobs, and they made it through some tough times. Later in life, when the time was right, her mother sat her and her sister and brother down and told them that they were now old enough to hear what happened to their father. In a way, at first, she didn't really want to know. She hadn't had a lot of memories of him. She would fantasize that he would ride back into town and save them from their poverty and despair. Sometimes, at night, she tried to remember what he looked like. The best she could do was to look at her brother. He didn't look as much like her mom, so he must look like her dad.

Her mother explained that sometimes people, her father possibly, do bad things. They then go away to sit it out or let things cool down, so to say, away from the location where the deed was done. As was common with criminals or people who were avoiding the law, they arrive in a remote western state and settle into a life of small-town America. Not knowing that her husband was a man to be hiding out, she fell hook, line, and sinker for this fellow from back east. He had a story of wanting to live in the west, and there was no reason to doubt what he said. He courted her, proposed marriage, set up house, and started a family. He went to work at her father's sawmill and was a skilled and good worker. Things were okay in their marriage. They didn't fight, and he never was mean to her.

After he had been away from the east where he came from for ten years, he just picked up lock, stock, and barrel and left. He didn't take anything but some clothes and a few personal items. No note or letter was left. Nothing.

This is why her mother cried every night. She hadn't known any of this when he left. She was devastated by being abandoned. She hadn't done anything wrong and was not deserving of this treatment. She was able to get a divorce on grounds of abandonment. It was many years later she discovered where he had gone.

So the young girl became a young wife, made a good home, had a family, and she and her husband never discussed her father. They, as a young couple, bought a run-down motel. They put their heart and soul into it and fixed it up into a really quaint place for travelers to stop and spend the night. They converted one of the rooms into a cute little coffee shop and TV room and served continental breakfast to the guests who chose to partake. This business helped them make a living to raise their family. They were fortunate to have a lot of friends who came to visit, have a cup of coffee and sweet roll, and watch TV.

Many years later, something happened that made her think a lot of her father. A younger man and his elderly mother stopped to rent a room. She was happy to rent them a room with two large beds, and he paid her in cash. One-night stay turned into another and then a week. Every day he paid for another night's stay in cash. It didn't take too long for her to notice that they really didn't have a lot of clothes; each was wearing the same thing every day. He wore a black suit, white shirt, and very polished shoes. His mother had a black knee-length dress with jacket, a huge broach on her collar, and expensive rings on her fingers. They were always showered and clean, but mostly looked like they just came from a funeral.

Her husband and she had nice conversations with them while sharing a coffee and sweet roll. The travelers asked lots of questions about the rural community, the western way of life, and what sights to go see. But they never went out. They stayed at the motel day after day. After two weeks of the day-to-day visits, the young man renting the room each night and paying in cash, she invited them for dinner. They eagerly accepted, and they had a lovely meal and conversation. The man asked them if he could rent the room on a weekly basis. They of course had never had anyone stay more than three days, so this was all new to them. They gave them a weekly rate, and he paid up front in cash.

After a few days, it became obvious to her that they just might need a laundry service and a few personal items. She hit them up over coffee and the TV watching and asked if she could help out in any way. Not wanting to be separated, the young man gave her a list of a few items and gave her more than enough cash to pay for them. When she returned, she gave them the items and change. He refused to take the money and told her it was her tip. Needless to say, it was the largest tip she had ever received—enough to buy a week's groceries. So she took it. She made sure she provided extra items to them for their comfort and invited them to dinner three to four times a week.

They stayed the entire summer. Each week had him paying in cash. Her husband and she talked together several times about the strangeness of the situation. He said not to question it, as of now they were guests on a different path than their own. The steady money was wonderful. It was a great summer for the motel, and they were able to get TV installed in each of the rooms. The guests were grateful for that, but still came to chat, read the paper, and drink coffee in the coffee room.

Fall was beginning to turn the leaves gold, and there seemed to be restlessness in the young man. He seemed somewhat nervous but did not reveal that anything was wrong. One day he asked her husband if he knew anything about Canada. They talked, and he seemed eager to learn some information. Three days later, they were gone. Just like that. They left in the middle of the night without a hint that they were going. When she went to clean their room, it was as tidy as a pin. You would never know that this mother and son had been staying in this room for four and a half months. While changing the bed that the old woman had been sleeping in, she found $500 in one-hundred-dollar bills lying under the pillow. On top of it, written in shaky writing on the wrapper of a facial soap provided in the bathrooms, was "Difficult roads lead to beautiful destinations." She knew it wasn't left by mistake. It was left for her and her husband for their hospitality. It was a huge amount of money for them. During those times, it was a windfall.

The one nagging question that she thought of a lot after their departure was what were they doing? It came to her soon, and she was reminded of her father leaving, and she then believed that these two men must have had similar past lives.

As she and her husband talked about the young man and his mother, she broke down and talked about her father and the abandonment and hurt. They comforted each other and promised that if anyone came asking about the couple, they would reveal nothing. It's not like they had a lot to reveal, they just provided a place to stay for two travelers who had a difficult road to go. They spent their lifetime running the motel and never again had guests who were quite like the young man and his mother.

It's a funny thing how a soft sound can bring back so many memories. So as they strolled and talked and discovered this new path to walk on, the old woman's words came to her again. Her difficult childhood was turned into a good and happy life. The piece of paper was tucked down in her dresser drawer as it was a cherished reminder of her life and the summer she met some guests. In her head, she said again, "Difficult roads lead to beautiful destinations." Indeed they do, and she squeezes her husband's hand a little tighter.

4

A Promise Kept

BLUE BIRDS ARE IN THE park today. The males are so pretty blue, and the females a drab gray. They remind me of change in the spring. Spring is a time of prosperity and renewal—new beginnings. I enjoy seeing the birds and feeling the change in the air at this time of year.

Walking toward me is a young married couple. Their two-year-old son is being carried by the grandfather while the child's father pushes an empty stroller. I say hello and get return hellos from them all.

The young husband was raised by his father, the grandfather, alone, as his mother died of ovarian cancer when he was very young. His mother was devoted to his father and him as a child and was devastated by her diagnosis. As she battled her cancer, his father was ever diligent by her side and tended to her every need.

As she neared the end, they had conversations about the raising of their son. She asked her husband to remarry if he found love. She wanted her only child to have a mother in this world, as she would watch over him in another world. Her husband refused to hear of it! He stated matter-of-factly that he would raise his son by himself. He promised her that he would solely raise the boy and he would not marry another to raise his and her child.

His promise was repeated every time she mentioned the subject. He was a man of his promises and this one he intended to keep to the love of his life. He would kiss her and profess his love to her every time she woke, as she lay in bed for weeks until she passed on.

He being the man that he is was dedicated to his son. Never a day went by that he didn't interact with the child. Everything was sports with the man. The child and he would throw balls, catch Frisbees, shoot baskets, kick balls, ride bikes, practice racing each other, and play croquet. In the winter, they snowshoed, went sledding, skied, went ice-skating, bowled, played Ping-Pong, and played hockey. The boy's two favorite sports ended up being basketball and hockey. He started young, so he became good at an early age.

Ever his number one fan, his father was at every event. During the school year or summer, his dad was always in the stands or on the sideline. And boy was he! You could hear him throwing out advice and shouting and clapping and hoot and hollering during the entire event. It was embarrassing to the boy sometimes because his dad was so vocal. He wished sometimes that he wouldn't come, but when he saw the kids on his team who didn't have anyone there to support them, he felt bad about feeling that way. Still, there were times when his dad went overboard. He didn't only comment about how his son was playing, he commented on everyone's play. This, of course, angered other parents and fans. His dad got into verbal altercations with other adults sometimes, and this was very embarrassing to his son.

One time, he and another father almost came to blows. They were both ejected from the gym. His dad was waiting in the truck when the game was over. He said he was sorry that he let his emotions get the best of him. He promised to not do that again, and as a man of his word, he never got kicked out of another sporting event.

The father knew from that point on just how far he could push it before he was over the line. He almost always pushed it right to the line. When the young boys would say, "Your dad is intense." or "Boy, your dad seems mad all the time.", he would cover for him and respond that he, his son, was all that he had and he was probably mad at God because his mother wasn't there.

He had felt for a long time that his dad vented at his games, not because of what the team was doing or not doing, but from inner personal frustration. He knew his dad filled his life with sports to cover for the void in his personal life.

As the young man got older and into high school, he felt sorry for his dad being all by himself when all the other young men had two parents at the team dinners and year-end award ceremonies. The young man had a great personal coach in his dad and excelled with his hockey. When his father was asked to chair the hockey parents support group, he was flattered and accepted. His position was a positive thing for many supporters. However, he had his distractors. It was as if you either loved the guy or you hated him. It was a good thing that he had more lovers than haters. The dad was very active and involved with the boy's hockey program, and the program flourished. Many fun events and trips were had during the boy's high school years. The team was successful and won many titles.

When graduation time came, the son accepted a hockey scholarship. His father was happier than his son, he believed. His father was as proud as any man could be. He loved his son so much and was bursting with respect and pride. When people would come up to the father and tell him what a great son he had and what a great athlete his son was, he was humbled. He would tell them that the boy was more like his mother as he had her personality. He would thank them and tell them that he and his wife were the proudest parents. People might have thought that was odd for him to talk about his wife this way, when she had died when the boy was so young. What they didn't know was that she was watching over him and had been there every step of the way.

In college, he had a fantastic career with his hockey. Again, his dad was at every game. They would spend hours talking about the other teams and the professional hockey clubs. They had a very tight bond. During his junior year, he met a girl who also came from an athletic background. She had played volleyball, basketball, track and field, and had one year of golf in high school. She had accepted a scholarship to play volleyball at the university he also attended. She was a standout on the team and a very good student also.

They hit if off pretty well; but with their studies, practices, training, and games, they had little time to spend together. If they did have some free time, they would go to watch some sporting event on campus. After graduation, both with their degrees, they became serious about finding jobs. His degree was in business management and hers in sociology. He was fortunate to find a job at the university with the sports athletic department in the business office. It was a dream job for him. She on the other hand had a few hits and misses with finding the perfect job. When she decided to apply at an assisted living facility and work with the elderly, she knew she had found the job for her. Every day she learned so much from working with the greatest generation. How quick-witted and knowledgeable the men were was something she enjoyed being part of. The women were tough—inner tough. They had little in their lives and made the best of it. Most of them had amazing stories to be told. She very much liked her work.

When things were established with both the young people's jobs, they had a romance ending in proposal and marriage. Of course, he proposed at a sporting event. That hockey game was exciting from the beginning with his father on one side of her and he on the other. While sitting on the bleachers, she was tapped on the shoulder from a hockey fan sitting behind her. The fellow, whom she did not know, handed her a dozen roses. She asked what was going on and the guy said, "I'm just the wingman." She looked to her boyfriend, and he and his dad both got down on one knee and asked her if she would marry us! She said, "Us?" He said, "Yes, me and my dad. We are a team, and we want you to be part of it." Of course she said yes, and they married soon after.

When they knew she was pregnant and broke the news to his father, the father was beyond happy. His hope would be to be as much in his grandchild's life as he could be. The baby was born early spring and was a boy. They gave him two famous hockey greats' first names and hoped this boy would follow in the footsteps of his father. He was a robust child and was learning to throw a ball at a very early age.

One day her father-in-law was sipping coffee and reading the sports section in the local paper. She approached a subject she and her husband had discussed together. She said, "Dad," (he told her to call him that as she was the daughter he never had) "I have something to talk to you about." He was all attention. "You know how you promised your wife that you would raise my husband on your own?"

"Yes."

"You did a fine job, and he is a wonderful husband and father. You went beyond the call of duty to raise him with your promise, but, Dad, your job is done. It's time you got on with the rest of your life. You don't need to fulfill any more days of being alone. I'm not saying to get into a deep committed relationship. How about just friendship or companionship? Spending time with someone your own age who has experienced loss or left an unfulfilling relationship? Maybe going to a sporting event or dinner? Finding someone you can share common interests with? What do you think, Dad? Will you consider it?"

He thought a minute and said that yes, he had fulfilled his promise as his wife was the love of his life. He had not wavered from his promise, and yes, he had fulfilled it. As he looked at his dear, sweet, daughter-in-law, he could hear his wife say that he should marry again if he found love. He knew he couldn't do that, but he could maybe have a female friend. He told his daughter-in-law that he would try. She said, "Will you, really?" He then looked at her and said he would try very much to have a friend or companion. He promised. He then said, "I am a man of my word, and when I make a promise, I keep it." She hugged him and told him that it would be easier than he believed. After all, she said, she already knew a few older ladies who just might like to go to a sporting event.

Today in the park is a spring of new beginnings, a time to let the past lie and move in a new direction with a promise of spring and a promise not broken.

5

It's in the Cards

IT IS VERY WINDY TODAY. It makes me think how nature planned it to be windy in the spring and the fall. I was told once that the wind moves the trees to move the sap up in the spring and down to the roots in the fall. Sounds like divine intervention to me. A lot of things in nature are amazing. The wind is used in this case as a tool of change.

I know on days like this there are not very many people walking. Hearing the old oaks creak and pop with the wind makes you watchful for anything falling from way up high.

A group is trying to set up a balloon bouncy house for some sort of function, and the wind is giving them fits. They scurry around tying things down and getting supplies out of trucks, and it makes me smile as it reminds me of the busy squirrels.

I pass two elderly women who are ambling along. They acknowledge me with a nod as I say hello.

They have been friends for years and know each other very well. With the recent death of one of their husbands, they now have a closer bond than ever. A person cannot know what another person is going through until you experience it yourself. So lately, they have spent quite a bit of time together. When a man was a difficult person, his passing can sometimes seem as a blessing. A wife feels some relief, then guilt for feeling like that. She knows he wasn't always difficult, in fact quite the opposite. He was kind and generous with her.

As a very young couple, they didn't have much money. There was enough to pay the bills, but not a lot left once they contributed to their retirement. Over the years they didn't buy each other gifts for the holidays. They always exchanged cards only. They would sit on the couch and each open their card and either laugh or cry for the sentiment inside. She would surely miss getting cards from her husband in the future. When he first had symptoms of prostate cancer, he chocked it up to old age and it being just the way it is. After they found out he had the cancer, it changed him emotionally. He became bitter and angry. She felt that her calm, kind husband had flown out the window, and this new "Get off my lawn!" angry old guy had replaced him. She felt terrible that the dreams they shared when they lay out in the back of his pickup truck under the night sky stars were mostly accomplished, but not all. They would do this lying out as their so-called cheap date. Living out on a farm, it was easy to see the night sky and the stars. Living in the city doesn't provide this opportunity to see it. Not having a lot of money to go to the movies or eat out, they would take a few beers and a quilt and pillows and drive out on a dirt road and lay in the back of the truck. They talked and planned and dreamed and laughed and cried and prayed. It bonded them together for life. These cheap dates are one of her fondest memories of their early life together. He also brought the memory up over the years as he too cherished this time they had in their early lives.

They had planned to travel at the age they are now, and it would have been one of the major things on their bucket list. It wouldn't happen now for her being alone. When he got ill, she felt the loneliness and knew that she would be alone forever. Little did she know that the feeling of loneliness would grip her long before his death. When the end was near and he was hospitalized, she was surrounded by family and friends. They helped her to focus on the man he once was and not the man he was toward the end of his life. It doesn't matter how many visits you get or phone calls or functions she goes to; she was now always alone at night.

On this day, the two women were talking about going through his things. Her friend, having done this with her husband's possessions, said that as she was trying to figure out what to do with his stuff, she came up with the idea to bring her joy throughout the year. She found the letters tied up with strings that she had written to her husband when he was in the service. He had saved every one. She said reading these old letters makes her feel young again and very happy. As she had also saved all the letters that he wrote to her, she was able to put them in order. First a letter she wrote to him, then his letter to her in response; back and forth with a letter from each other until he was discharged from military duty and returned home. That's when the letters stopped.

She said she loves reading them, and when she starts feeling lonely and misses him, she pulls out the letters, reads the words, daydreams about those years so long ago, and she transports herself to a happier time. This fills her with much joy.

The new widow's response was that she didn't have letters to read, but she had stacks of cards that were saved from all the years they gave cards to each other. She also had cards from relatives, children, and friends.

Her memory flashed to the special cards he gave her and how over the years his handwriting had gotten shaky, but his "I love you" meant just as much.

As they continued to walk and talk, she said that she could display the cards for each holiday just like she did years ago when she got a card. It would be a big display, as a lot of cards had been received over the years. The friend suggested that they first organize the cards by holiday or occasion, and as each holiday or occasion was coming up, she could display the cards on the mantel, tables, dressers, and most of all, the dining room table. After the holiday or occasion was over, she could take them all down and put up the next set of cards.

She really liked this idea and knew how welcoming it would be to wake from her lonely nights in bed, and she would be greeted by the cards, she cherished and gave her joy.

Her friend then said words to her that made her know that until she died, she would display the lovely cards her husband had hand-picked for her each time. "Do not mourn what is lost, instead rejoice at what was." She hugged her friend and asked her to come over and help her organize the cards by holiday and occasion. She wanted it to get done before the next holiday, which was Father's Day. So they would have to scurry around like the busy squirrels and laugh and cry at the sentiments on the cards. In her heart she would feel better that although life has to end, love doesn't.

6

False Spring

TODAY, WALKING IS A PLEASANT surprise as the temperatures are way above normal for spring. In the movie *The Shootist*, John Wayne is encouraged at how warm it is, as he has just arrived in town, and is informed that this unseasonably warm weather is called a false spring. Later in the movie, he takes a buggy ride with Loren Bacall, and she exclaims how nice the weather is. John then happily tells her that it is a false spring. It pleases him that he is knowledgeable of such things, even though it was just recently learned.

I feel the warmth of the false spring and have to remove my jacket and tie it around my waist. I hear voices behind me and stop to let the faster walkers pass me up. Two young women who appear to be friends say hello back to me as I say my hello and let them pass.

This friendship is friendly only on the outside for all to see. The true relationship is truly false and not a healthy one at all. Little does the shorter woman know that her friend is, as Dr. Phil has explained to us all, a baiter. As open as she is with her thoughts, ideas, dreams, and experiences with her friend, she has no idea of the darker ugly fact that her husband is sleeping with her walking partner.

Both husbands work together at a successful body and paint shop. They became friends and then fishing buddies many years ago. Over the course of time, both couples enjoyed many outings together and planned fishing, camping, and holiday barbecues together. The shorter woman has two young children who keep her very busy. The other has no children or job and says she really enjoys her friendship and being around the children as she has none of her own. She has convinced the mother that she would love a child, but it's a lie. She wouldn't put her perfect figure through a pregnancy or tie herself into the full-time attention a child would require. She doesn't feel guilty at all for what she is doing, it's just sex. There's no love involved. It started out as a flirtation that just developed into the weekly Tuesday lunchtime tryst. Her husband runs the crew at work and takes a road trip every Tuesday to go to the capitol city to pick up parts, paint, and supplies and to sometimes help out the sister business in that city.

After bumping into the husband at a summer barbecue while getting more ice for her drink in the kitchen, she ran her hand down his chest and commented that she thought he was handsome. He had always thought she was pretty and very sexual. Her comment hit him off guard, and he responded with interest. One thing said led to another, and the plan was set for him to visit on his lunch hour the next Tuesday at her house. No Gladys Kravitz neighbor would be suspicious of his truck in her driveway as he came over to her house all the time. It was common for him to park his vehicle at her place while he rode with her husband on some adventure or outing.

Everything happened as planned, and the rendezvous just kept happening. He told her that he just didn't get enough sex from his wife anymore as the children put a damper on their sex life. She was perfectly fine with this as he wasn't the first guy she seduced during her marriage. She had always loved the thrill of the hunt, seeking out willing men, and she celebrated herself about being able to conquer them. Neither of them thought anything about what would happen if they got caught. As with a false spring, so is this false friendship. It looks good for the moment, but there are darker days ahead.

I watch the backsides of the chatty women as they walk away from me and laugh at myself for thinking of John Wayne today. He was a man's man. I thought he was handsome with his scarves, vests, and cowboy class. He had a gentle side to him with his mannerisms and the way he looked at and spoke to women. I liked that in him. He was the real deal, not fake. Not false at all.

7

Remodeling Surprise

I HAD THINGS TO DO this morning, so I did not get to walk until the afternoon. There are more young students at this time of day as they must come to run the trails for the sports they participate in at their schools or college. This is a pretty athletic city with lots of sport programs. With football, volleyball, wrestling, basketball, tennis, hockey, baseball, soccer, swimming, and skiing programs, a person can stay busy year-round attending sporting events.

I don't walk real fast as arthritis in my hips and right ankle makes me walk at a comfortable pace, but not speed walk. If I push it, I really pay for it the next day. Not one to take medications for aches and pain, I walk through my stiffness as my remedy. A body in motion works for most of my aches.

I am approached by a woman who I know is not a serious walker. She does not have the sports clothing that all the younger people wear. She is not even wearing tennis shoes. I'm pretty sure that this walk is a get-out-and-catch-your-breath stroll to think and calm down. As I pass her and say hello, I can tell she is a good person as she responds with a hello and asks me for the time. I look at my phone, and she laughs when I tell her. She states that she needs to go home as she needs to watch her two granddaughters. I tell her I enjoy watching my granddaughters and ask her how old hers are. She says two and four and states that they are a handful but she loves them so. I know the feeling, and she moves on after saying goodbye.

She's had a tough couple of months. What was supposed to be a simple project has turned into an ongoing financial pain in the neck. After her mother died, her parents' house was put on the market to be sold and the proceeds divided by herself and her three brothers. Most everything went smoothly, and she got a nice little settlement from her parents' estate. After stewing on it for quite a while over conversations with her husband, she decided to spend the money on a remodel of her kitchen. It would be a lovely tribute to her parents as they were great entertainers and excellent cooks. Every meal was wonderful; nothing store-bought from them. There are so many memories of the happiest of days and holidays with food being prepared and eaten. So with an idea in mind, she contacted a contractor and told him her budget. Replacing the cupboards, countertops, flooring, appliances, and light fixtures, her inheritance was all but spent. She was surprised at how much everything cost, but felt the investment into her home would add good value. She said okay and asked how long it would take to finish the project. The contractor felt he could be finished by Christmas, and she was ecstatic to get going on this project so her house would look great for the holidays.

She has had her daughter and granddaughters living with her and her husband since the untimely death of her son-in-law in Afghanistan. Nothing can prepare a family for the loss of a husband, father, son, son-in-law, and uncle. To make it all the more tragic, her son-in-law never got to meet his youngest daughter. As family, you do what you don't know you can do at a time like that. So in giving it all they could give, they opened their home for their daughter and her girls to come and reside and get their footing. In a military city, there is a lot of support, but the day-to-day was placed on her and her husband. It was a challenge at first but very rewarding to be with the little girls. They just make you smile and laugh. Her daughter decided to go back to college after a year, so she was now the full-time, part-time, unpaid, most important grandma babysitter. Her husband stayed busy at work and never verbalized any discontent about these events except to her as they lie in bed. Mostly he expressed confusion as to why his daughter didn't make more of an effort to help his wife with the girls or household tasks. She always responded that the daughter would come around, just give her time. Lately the daughter was gone longer than normal, and they adjusted to her being gone. It would have been easier if the kitchen was done, but her attitude was "all things in time."

The contractor started work the first part of December and immediately destroyed the kitchen. The stove and oven were still usable, and the fridge was now plugged into the dining room. She was able to put all the cupboard items in boxes in the utility room and move things in and out from there. The sink was supposed to be usable until the new one would be set in the new countertop, but unforeseen by anyone, they ran into a huge snag. While removing cupboards and flooring, it was discovered that black mold was very much present from leaking old pipes. This is not something you can avoid, and the contractor explained how everything would have to come out and be replaced. To say the least, her budget just went out the window. With all the removal and replacement, he said he would not have it completed by Christmas. As optimistic as she is, she said okay and mentally thought of how great it would be next Christmas. Inside, however, she felt like screaming. They made the best out of the circumstances. Christmas was fun with the girls, and everyone prayed that the New Year would get them out of this mess. The cost ran high, so they got a home equity line of credit loan and used her inheritance as a safety net for expenses. It wasn't what was planned, but she and her husband felt the investment into the house was worth it. There were a lot of delays, and just the inconvenience of not having a fully functioning kitchen was stressful. Tempers were starting to flare, and her husband had words with their daughter that morning. He looked around his once-tidy, well-kept home at all of the chaos and said to his daughter, while stepping over more toys than he had ever had in his whole life as a child, "Do you know what you're doing to your mother?" Why he said this was a shock to her, and the mom could have died. She couldn't believe he was taking the frustration he was feeling and putting it all on her plate. The daughter said, "No, Dad, I don't have time for this shit." Then she slammed the door and went to class. The mom just broke down and cried. He walked over and gave her a hug and apologized. She said she would talk to their daughter this afternoon and that she would make a nice supper and for him to have a nice day and that she loved him. He kissed her and said he loved her too. He kissed each little girl and did the grandpa bear growl hug to make each girl giggle and hug him back.

So with that, she cleaned and tidied and baked and waited for her daughter. A little after two, her daughter came in and kissed her girls, threw some leftovers in the microwave (which was on the kitchen table), and sat down to eat a late lunch.

While the girls were napping, she thought now was the time to talk. She got a cup of coffee and sat down with her daughter. One look at her, and she knew that something was heavy on her daughter's heart. Before she could gather up what to ask and to avoid a confrontation, her daughter blurted out, "Mom, I'm pregnant."

Talk about getting hit by a ton of bricks. This is the last thing they needed. Stuttering with bewilderment, she spits out, "Who, how, and why?" The story rolled out among the sobs. He was a student, very nice, one thing led to another, no protection, she's two months along.

Sometimes maturity slaps us in the face during unexpected times. She got up and hugged her daughter, reassured her that everything would be okay and that this must be God's plan. The mom knew her husband would blow a gasket, but would be the best grandpa to another grandchild. With that thought, she excused herself and told her daughter that she needed some time to think and that she wanted to get outside. Her daughter didn't have class until later, so she left to walk and pray and wish and ask the Lord what to do. She knew the answer. It was all going to be okay.

As I continue walking, I think about how young these students are and how the things they do right now affect so many other people. I say a prayer for them to be safe and responsible to their schools, communities, and mostly to their families.

I then think of my grandchildren and wonder what they will be like grown up. I just hope that I have longevity in life to see who they become. If not, I know that they will all be in the plan and it all is going to be okay.

8

Bullied Victory

Today I see another kind of bird in the park. There are robins everywhere. It would be interesting to know where they will end up spending the summer. I'm not sure if they mate for life. They symbolize joy and a sense of renewal, such a happy thought and feeling. With the first signs of spring, it is appropriate to see all these birds today.

Running toward me is a man younger than me but not by a lot. He is handsome and in terrific shape. He has a lovely smile and says howdy when I say hello. He reminds me of my brother, and that thought makes me smile.

He is running in the park today to enjoy getting outdoors and taking in the sights and sounds of spring and the renewal of the earth. His life as a child was very hard as he and his sister and his mom had a rough go of it. They were poor, even though his mom worked a lot as a waitress. There just wasn't money to go around for any extras. He remembers one school year in grade school they did not have money for new shoes. His sister was given hand-me-downs from the neighbors and had two pair of shoes. One leather pair and one white tennis shoe pair. His mother gave him the tennis shoes to wear, and he didn't mind doing so, until the kids on the bus and at school noticed and started bullying and teasing him. They were relentless about making fun of him and his sister and their clothes. It didn't help any that he had a very funny last name either. They made up little ditties and used his last name in it, to constantly keep the bullying up.

His childhood gave him a good foundation on what he didn't want in life. He struggled in school and did not get good grades. He was sick a lot and missed a lot of school, which didn't help his grades. His mom would save his papers in a box, and each summer when his aunt and uncle came to visit, his uncle would go through them and work with him. His uncle was a schoolteacher in another state, and his visit each year was a highlight of the summer. Maybe it was because he was a kind man, or maybe it was that his frame of mind was different, but the learning sessions were productive. Subjects like math and spelling made more sense the way his uncle taught him.

Doing better in school didn't help his self-esteem once school started. He couldn't change his last name, but getting better grades eliminated the bullies from calling him *stupid* and *idiot*. He grew real tall and was encouraged to join the swim team at school. His mom worked extra shifts on Saturdays so she could pay his swim team fees. He did real well and found that with success with winning swimming events, his self-confidence improved a lot.

One day he was complaining to his mom about not having new clothes to go on a swim meet trip. His mother reminded him that he could be mad and upset about what he didn't have or be thankful for what he did have. He hugged her and thanked her for working so hard for him to be able to participate in the swim club. She told him that his life would not always be difficult if he aspired to have it better. He promised he would win for her that day, and he left with a new joy and sense of renewal. He did win one of his races that day. He participated in three, and one out of three wasn't so bad.

His uncle continued to come every summer, and he benefitted from their special bond and the way he taught him. His grades were improving, and his self-esteem grew leaps and bounds. At one point, he turned the tables on the kids who continued to bully him about his last name. He would start laughing when they were trying to make him feel bad. They saw him saying things like "It's a weird name, but it's mine, and I'm used to it." He would say his name out loud and follow it with "I am going to be somebody someday." The bullies didn't have much delight when he did this, and they turned their attention to other less-fortunate kids to bully. In high school, he was asked to be a lifeguard and was proud to have been asked. He was serious about the job and ever watchful of all the young swimmers. He could pick out the bullies and their victims very quickly. The look on a victim's face was always a look of terror saying "This bully is going to drown me!" He had no tolerance for this behavior, and he would kick the bullies out of the pool. The first time, they had to sit out for half an hour, but if he caught them terrorizing anyone again, he would expel them from the pool. The little swimmers who had been harassed were so thankful and loved him.

As he finished up his high school years, he decided to go to college rather than the military. He just felt that the boot camp experience would be too much like bullying, and he did not need to go back to that negativity and sadness again in his life.

He had good grades to go and was honored for his well-rounded high school years for being in swim club and being a lifeguard. With a few scholarships and financial aid, he decided to go into the medical programs. There was no one prouder than his uncle when he graduated. For all his care and concern, had brought forth fruit, and it was exciting.

He knew he owed a lot to his mom and vowed he would work hard, get a good job, and help her out financially. He was successful with his plan and was fortunate to find employment as a physician's assistant. His first priority was to help his mom and his sister out. He owed so much to his mom for her advice to be thankful for what he has and not to be upset about what he didn't have.

At work he often had people snicker or laugh at his last name. He would smile and agree that it sure was crazy, but he was used to it. One day he looked at the day's list of patients and saw the name of a man who had been one of the worst bullies when he was young. Seeing his name made him feel funny inside, and a little nervous. He managed to calm himself and tend to the patients he had ahead of this man, and his morning flew by with all that he had to do.

When the appointment time arrived, he took a deep breath, ran his fingers through his thick hair, straightened his shoulders to look as tall as ever, and opened the door to the room. With the first look, he saw the man the young bully had turned into. He reached out his hand for a handshake to an overweight, balding, unkempt man with grease under his nails, in bad need of a proper shave and haircut.

He said hello and asked how he was doing today. The man said "Hello, Doc" and that he couldn't believe it when he made the appointment and they said that it would be with a guy with his last name. He had wondered if it was him and laughed because he didn't think there were too many people with the same name as the doctor. At that moment, the physician's assistant had the most overpowering feeling of success being the sweetest revenge. He felt more confident than he had ever felt, and for the first time in his life, he felt sorry for the man. Not so sorry for what he looked like now, but sorry that he was so shallow as a child that his way of dealing with others was to bully them.

He asked the man why he was there and heard about how poorly the man was feeling. Taking extra care to examine him and ask every question under the sun in order to know about his life and habits, he then ordered up tests that would give him a better picture of what was going on.

They chatted about what they did after high school and some other people in their class. Throughout the whole conversation, the physician's assistant felt that there was sadness in this man. He hadn't amounted to anything much in his life. He was a mechanic but had little to be proud of. He had worked for many businesses and didn't find much happiness in what he did as he felt it was just a job. He had married and divorced. He said that his wife took him to the cleaners, and he didn't have a dime to his name. He had two kids whom he never saw and owed back child support for.

As the physician's assistant listened to him, he drew the comparison of reversal of fortune. What he had as a child with severe poverty and being looked down upon for struggling in school, this man who had made so much fun of him now had. He had not wished or prayed for it, it just happened. He now felt that the Lord works in mysterious ways. Here before him was a man he hated as a child and who now was in need of his help.

Someone petty or selfish would not have been able to forget the childhood indiscretions. He was better than that, and he would try with all he had been taught to help his health problems.

After the man fasted the next day, they had taken blood, some of the paperwork came back, and with the symptoms the man was experiencing, they determined that the man had a heart issue. A blockage was very likely. His cholesterol, blood pressure, liver enzymes, and diabetes levels were all out of bounds. He was a time bomb ready to detonate.

So the work began to fix this man. Physically he needed a lot. Emotionally he also needed work done. The physician's assistant passed him to a surgeon, and a blockage was found. Surgery was done, and with medications, they were able to get the high blood pressure, high cholesterol, and diabetes issues under control.

Many months later, he had a follow-up visit with this man. He was not his primary caretaker and was surprised to see his name on the list of patients that day. When the appointment time came, he took a deep breath, ran his fingers through his thick hair, straightened his shoulders to look as tall as ever, and opened the door to the room.

There sat a man he knew but who had changed. They shook hands, and he read the chart. He asked how he was and why he was there today. As the bully explained all that had happened since last they met, he told him that he was only here to thank him for the help. He then said that he owes him an apology for the years of terrorizing him and that he felt bad at how he acted when he was a kid.

The physician's assistant then said something that shocked him. He said, "Thank you for teaching me patience to get through the tough times, and thank you for letting me not be ashamed of who I was or what my name was or what my position in life was. I am a better person today for having the childhood that I had."

They shook hands, and the man was teary-eyed when he left.

Today as the physician's assistant runs, he does so to stay in good health because he sees a lot of neglect people do to their bodies in his line of work. He enjoys the work he does, and he enjoys the life his life has become. He has to hurry up his run and get showered to go out to lunch today with a sweet girl he knows who laughs with him about his last name and thinks he is one good-looking guy with a great head of hair. He smiles at that thought. He is ready for the next step of his life, like the robins he sees today, getting ready to start something new.

Cat Tale

AFTER ATTENDING CHURCH TODAY, MY husband and I decided on this fine Easter Sunday morning to take a walk as we are having our large meal later in the day. The park is full of families setting up Easter egg hunts for children who are very excited. Everyone is happy and most are in springtime Easter colored dresses and shorts. Many families will barbecue and picnic, and the smell of the barbecue pits starting and the cooking of ribs, chicken, and hot dogs begins to fill the air.

There are ladybugs on the path today, and I try really hard not to step on any. I have always loved the ladybug and know that they are good to have in your garden to eat the aphids. In some cultures, the ladybug is considered good luck. Another fun fact about them is that they symbolize to let things flow at a natural pace and have a keen instinct not to try too hard or go too fast.

So we stroll as we have no hurry today. There is a woman standing on the path watching two young children chase after bubbles blown into the air by their mother. The children have hunted for Easter eggs and are now having a very fun time with chasing the bubbles. She says hello as we pass, and we say, "Hello, happy Easter."

She is the aunt of the two young children. She has no intention of ever having children, so her niece and nephew are the closest she will come to having children in her life. She has been watching the children, but her mind is elsewhere. She shortly will tell her sister that she has enjoyed watching the children, but she wants to go home.

She now has a reason to go home as she just acquired a cat from the animal shelter, and her excuse is that she needs to check on him. Many years ago she had a cat as a companion, and the orange male tabby was a great friend for her. She never had human friends as most people would judge a book by its cover and not choose to get to know her. To be honest, let's say she got hit with the ugly stick. She struggled all her life with the issue of her looks. She had a very droopy eye, and the skin under it sagged, and she could do nothing to change it. This is how God made her. When she was a child in school, the other students would tease her, and not being really skinny, they made fun of her weight also. A lot of adults also assumed that she wasn't smart and wouldn't engage her in conversation. She had been passed over for most everything in school, and she had accepted her place in life. Her first cat gave her years of companionship, and she was devastated when she had to have him put down due to advanced age. She swore that never again would she go through that heartache. So for over twenty years, she was alone with no human or animal friend or companion, only having her sister in her life.

She had done well in school and graduated with honors and scholarships. Not being distracted in any way by friendships or social events, she dedicated herself to her studies. She then went to college. She didn't participate in the social college life and again made very good grades and got her degree. After a few failed attempts to work in an environment with office politics and unkind coworkers, she interviewed for the librarian job she holds to this day. Ideally she is able to work by herself in a quiet atmosphere and can counter the loneliness in her life by the adventures she can go on with the books she reads. She has a very simple life, so reading the stories of faraway places and people who have done amazing things fills most the voids except one. When she goes home at night after work, she is met by darkness and deathly quiet.

Just recently she was watching the news about the overabundance of animals that the humane society had for adoption. They were pleading with the community to please open their hearts and homes and give these dogs and cats a good home. It really pulled on her heartstrings, and she was reminded of her first and only cat and the love she shared with him. Being motivated by curiosity and community need, she figured it would not hurt to go take a look.

One day after work, she went to the humane society and asked if she could view the cats. She knew she didn't want a dog. Dogs needed to have daily exercise, and she being a heavy woman had no intention of walking a dog every day. The cat house part of the building was loaded with cats in cages. There were many kittens of all sizes up front and center for all to see. This was probably done purposefully to tug at your heartstrings, and she was sure they were successful with this marketing technique. The kittens were a hodge-podge of colors, and she thought they were all cute.

Some older male and female cats were down closer to the floor in their cages, and most were dozing or could care less who was looking in on them. Back in the corner, she spied an orange tabby and, with closer inspection, saw that it was a male. The way he was lying in the cage was just like her first cat! He was lying on his back with his legs out straight in both directions. It is the funniest position, and she laughed out loud. Her close laughter woke the cat, and he stirred, stretched, and came to the front of the cage. One look at him, and she knew he was in rough shape. He was missing the end of his tail, he had scars all over his face, and both ears had been frozen at some point and were now uneven nubs for ears. You could say that he got hit with the ugly stick. She asked the attendant about him and wanted to know his story.

She was told he got caught in a live trap. They know he was someone's cat at one time as he had been neutered. He was not a feral cat, he was cat box trained, and as far as his teeth showed, he was about three years old. He seemed very friendly and hadn't given any of the staff a problem at all. As far as they could guess, someone couldn't keep him, so they just put him out and probably moved. This is common more so than anyone would imagine, she was told.

Hearing that he was friendly, she put her fingers in to pull his whiskers as her first cat used to love her to do that. The cat responded to her touch and started this megaphone purring. This made her smile and laugh to herself as this also was like cat number one. She was told by her vet when she got her first cat that male orange tabbies have very neat personalities. For some reason, they are super social and all-around characters.

As she pulled the whiskers and scratched this cat's forehead, she just melted with memories and knew she needed to save this cat. Arrangements were made, and she bought a carrier and supplies. She paid for fees and the chip they put in him, and she left with her new friend. Not being able to name him on the spot, she told the attendant that she would call them with his name, so it would be on his chart after he had a name.

When she got home, she didn't feel that introducing him to the house to start with would be good. She set up a nice bedding area, food and drink area, and cat box area in the garage. When he first got let out of the cat carrier, he immediately began doing figure eights between her legs. She couldn't get him to stop until she reached down and picked him up. He then started the turbo purring. She was delighted with this, as it made her feel just plain happy inside. She played with him for a while and put him down by the food and went up the few steps to the house. She watched him through the door window for a while and then walked down the hall to her living room.

Later that evening, she decided she would name him Quasimodo, after the Hunchback of Notre Dame. This was because he looked bad on the outside, but was good on the inside, just like the hunchback of Notre Dame, and also like her.

Each day she let him come in the house for a short visit. He was really good and would curl up on the couch with her or wrap around her neck while she watched television. After a week, she moved his bed, food, and cat box inside the house. He now was her new housemate, and both couldn't be happier.

Each night she got home from work, he would greet her, and she would be so happy to have him to come home to. He brought her much joy. He could hear her car drive up, and as soon as she got in the door, he would be doing figure eights around her ankles. To even take a step, she had to put down her purse, groceries, or take-out dinner sacks and pick him up.

The blessing a pet gives us is unconditional love. They don't know if you have had a bad day. They are just so excited you are home. She found that her years of being afraid to love again had made her miss out on years of companionship and happiness.

As with the ladybugs who symbolize good luck and to not try and go too fast, she will take her time and enjoy every minute with her funny-looking, loving cat. So she tells her sister, niece, and nephew goodbye and heads home on this Easter day not knowing who saved who, but also knowing that they saved each other.

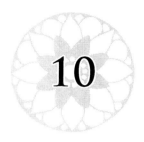

10

Thumper Theory

THERE WAS ANOTHER COLD SNAP of winter, and new snow covers everything in the park and on the trail. The beauty of the snow is how it covers up all ugliness and makes Mother Nature's world look so perfectly beautiful. It reminds me of a saying I always said to my children, that you can't just pretty up the outside of your appearance; you need to work on the inside of yourself so you are pretty on the inside. This was to get them to think about their personalities and the morals and values my husband and I raised them with.

I meet a young man making his way toward me, and I say hello. He walks pretty fast and has earbuds in, and he acknowledges me with a nod. He's walking to kill some lunch hour time and is not running the path today as there are slick spots with the new fallen snow.

He's been working at the insurance office since he graduated from college. He likes it pretty much except for one supervisor who is a very negative and sarcastic person. There has not been a day go by that he has not had to turn the other cheek because of this person's hateful comments. He pretty much has been made fun of for slowly learning his job, making mistakes, a new haircut, his tie, his older car, his writing, not wanting to participate in office politics, and his lack of a social life. It doesn't matter the topic of discussion, he gets a barb thrown his way if there is discussion in the office between the agents and staff. He really doesn't feel singled out all the time as others get the sharp-tongued supervisor's negative comments too!

Sometimes he has thought that this supervisor must be a miserable person on the inside. Maybe so insecure in his own skin that he dominates by hate-filled negativity. He has at a few points even felt sorry for him, but after the next slam to him, he would forget that thought. He often felt that he was damned if he did and damned if he didn't. There was no happy ground. So he worked quietly and did all the required work and oftentimes looked for extra things to do.

The agency was run by a very nice guy who was a terrific, funny guy. He liked him very much. That's why he stayed. Unfortunately, the head guy was clueless to the hate and discontent spilling from his supervisor. There had been complaints logged, but nothing had ever changed. One of the bad things about a supervisor is that an employee needs to log complaints by the chain of command, but if your complaint is against your direct supervisor, and they hear that you went over their head to the higher authority, then you were really on the shit list. Once this happens, there is vindictiveness and retaliation. He has experienced that, so he keeps his mouth shut and does his work and finds happiness in himself that he is doing the best of his ability and knows that this job is a stepping-stone to having his own business. So he knows he has to have longevity with this job and to learn all he can. He has a goal, and this quote from Steve Jobs keeps him motivated: "Your time is limited, so don't waste it living someone else's life. Don't be trapped by dogma—which is living with the results of other people's thinking. Don't let the noise of others' opinions drown out your own inner voice. And most importantly, have the courage to follow your heart and intuition."

With this positive motivation he can heal his hurt feelings and move forward as a positive person knowing that he will not fall prey to dish back negativity. His parents taught him to remember the Thumper Theory: If you can't say anything nice, then don't say anything at all.

He walks quickly to get back to the office so as to not clock in even one minute late, lest he get another negative comment from the supervisor who is pretty on the outside, but very ugly on the inside.

11

Life Dance

"HELLO," I SAY TO TWO older retired-age fellows who walk slowly and have been talking to each other the whole time as I approach. They both say hello, and one man states, "Hey, that's a nice jacket!" I wear a sports team warm-up jacket most cooler days and tell him thank-you, and he tells me he likes my team. We talk a little about who won and lost this past season and laugh about some of the crazy things a few of the athletes do. I then get on my way. As I make my way around the trail, I meet up with them sitting on one of the benches that are provided all along the trail. They are deep in conversation and again say hello to me. I am then told by one of them that I walk fast, but I laugh and say, "Not really, what with arthritis in my hips and ankle." I just walk at a comfortable pace. Little do I know the anguish of the quieter fellow who has a bedridden wife with severe arthritis. She has been bedridden for four years. He is her primary caretaker and gets a little break some days if the wife of his friend pushes him out the door to take a walk with her husband or if his daughter comes over to help him, which is a few times a week. He doesn't know what's in store for him and his wife, but he knows that getting out and strolling in this park helps lift his spirits. He sure would cherish a stroll with her again as in his memory she is as young and energetic and so full of life and fun.

They used to dance. Boy, did he look forward to the Saturday night dances. She was very light on her feet, and he wasn't so bad himself when it came to "cutting the rug," as they say. They even won the Best Dance Couple at a New Year's Eve dance a long time ago. The prize was a nice meal at a nice restaurant that he couldn't afford to take her but maybe once a year for her birthday. They really enjoyed the prize. Many times they were told by others what a handsome couple they were, and she would beam like the sun when they received this compliment.

Her pain and stiffness was mild at first, and they figured dancing and walking would stave it off, as she would get her juices flowing to her joints. Several years of things getting gradually worse, even with medications, put their dancing days on the back burner. What was once their main social activity had now become just a memory.

The thing that amazed him the most was how she didn't complain. Her attitude was lighthearted, just like her feather-light dance steps—so happy and carefree and graceful. She was in pain when they moved her to prevent the bedsores and to the bath and to change her. She would grimace and cry out, but would immediately replace it with a smile. This amazed him for her attitude to be so upbeat and positive. She told him time and time again that her hell was on earth and she would again one day have a perfect body. He hated it when she said that, but let her have her say and would say that he only wished he could take some of her pain, even if for one day. She would smile and thank him and remind him how much she loved him, and she would say she had to deal with this devil she knows, and he wasn't going to get the best of her. He may take her body, but not her spirit. What faith! What belief! He loved her for her strength, and she had no physical strength left. There is power in the mind.

He had watched people, athletes, children, accident victims—all overcome immense physical pain in their pursuit of a goal, whether it be on a movie or a sporting event. Little did he ever know that his wife would be one of them. The Lord gives you only as much as you can handle they say, and he was for some reason chosen to be the legs for the strength his wife had. Better than any athlete in training and working toward the super prize, she was going to make it, and he would be her number one cheerleader, and he needed to keep himself in shape as they were a team. Always were and always would be.

12

Hair Issues

AGAIN THE WEATHER IS COOL and breezy. It's not so bad when you're in the trees, but out in the open, it can be a bit gusty. Most walkers or joggers listen to music as they step along and do not hear the sound of the wind in the trees or the sounds of the city life. I hear the trains, sirens, and the school bell. There is the vehicle noise and, of course, the honking geese. There is a funny thing about the geese. I have drawn a comparison between them and humans. There really are several characteristics that both species have in common. Geese mate for life, and some people do the same. The proud gander watches out for his goose of choice while she sets and hatches her clutch, very much like a man's job of just being there during a woman's pregnancy. There isn't much he can do, but be by her side, as it's pretty much up to her to do the work. Once the eggs hatch, he gets a more active role and can be quite aggressive with anything that comes near her and his offspring. Men can be like that. Some are more mild-mannered, but most are very supportive to their newborn and wife. The gander struts with chest puffed out in his leadership role of leading his new family to greener pastures (let's say better grass) and, like men, stay on guard for all their safety. That's not much different than husbands and fathers being protective and the leader. A few ganders are very vocal. Let's say they never shut up. They constantly honk. Not all geese are like this. Only a few are constantly noisy.

Those on the trail wearing headphones do not hear any of this as they listen to a different beat with their music. I pass a woman who doesn't hear my hello due to headphones. She gives a half smile in acknowledgement and walks at a faster pace than me. I would guess her to be about my age with naturally thick and graying hair. It is wonderful to have thick hair at our age, as so many middle-aged women deal with thinning and sparse hair. She has had hair issues all her life. It started when she was a little girl, and her hair was so thick it would mat. Combing it out was painful, and she avoided doing a thorough combing until she had large matting, and her sisters had to help her. She was tender headed, and that was a problem. Her father would grab ahold of her in anger, and he always got a handful of hair and would yank so hard he would pull it out. She remembers that her childhood was not easy as one of five girls. She had her sisters to cling to, but each of them were living their own hell too. After a blowup with her dad, she would cry a lot as her sisters combed out the chunks of hair that they discarded in the trash. She would grow new hair, and it would come in as thick as ever. Then something or one of the sisters would do something to anger her father, and he would grab her and shake her and pull out some hair.

She was in second grade when her mother did what a mother is supposed to do and left him, finalizing a divorce. The joy was temporary as her mother remarried a fellow with different qualities than her father, but she had just as much stress. The stepdad was a clean freak, and a houseful of girls was all new to him. He quite frankly could not stand hairs on anything; most of all, not the floor. He would not ever touch her or the other girls, but they had the law laid down that his home would be clean and tidy, and God forbid if he found a hair on his sock, in his food, on the counter, in the bathroom, or on the floor. He threatened to cut her hair all off if he found hair. She remembers combing her hair over a towel so as to collect the loose hairs so she could shake it outside. She would vacuum a lot. But most of all, she would get down on her hands and knees and, with her fingers, scrape the tile and carpet to snag any loose hairs that she could collect. This was a twice-daily practice. There was always a lot of cleaning on the weekends, and nothing could be done until the house met his inspection. It was a form of living hell, but he never hit or touched her.

Of course she had beautiful thick hair, and she grew it very long. She was able to twist it up, or braid it, to minimize the hair falling out. She had a lot of compliments on the beauty of her hair, as no one knew the hell she had to go through daily to clean up after it.

One day when she was in ninth grade, she came to school with her hair bobbed short. All her friends and classmates were in shock as to why she had cut off her beautiful hair. She smiled and said she had gotten tired of it as it was a lot of work. Her sisters had sported shorter hairstyles for years. No one was told the truth as to the real reason her hair was bobbed. It was a scene right out of her nightmares. Her stepdad had his inspection, and he found hair. She had not had time to clean thoroughly as she had been to an interschool concert with her chorus class the day before and had gotten home late and tired. The bus trips are wonderful fun, and she had a great time, but it left little time for cleaning as she was gone a whole day.

The writing was on the wall. She knew the price she would pay if his standard was not kept. So he demanded her mother chop it off, and her mom did so, full of sadness knowing that, again, her daughter was being terrorized and her hair was being sacrificed.

She survived and left her home the minute she graduated. Old habits die hard, and she kept a very tidy, clean apartment. Over the years, she married, divorced, had a son, and went on to do well with the school system helping children in the preschool programs. One of the lessons she learned many years ago was that only she was responsible for her own joy. If joy was to be in her life, she had to let it in. So her life was filled with music. Every room had a sound system to listen to. She sang to every song on the radio. Even now, forgetting words to some songs, she will still sing. Singing and listening to music replaced some of the ugliness that had happened to her. It was time killing and time-consuming. What a gift she gave to herself to heal the noise of others' angry voices with the music to create calm and happiness. As she walks, she listens and sings silently to her special play mix, and she doesn't hear the world around her or the honking of the noisy ganders.

13

Stroller Plans

THE SQUIRRELS IN THE PARK are very busy creatures. They spend most all the fall gathering and burying the acorns they find. They don't pay any attention to the walking and running individuals as they are on a mission to bury the acorns everywhere. I don't know how many calories are in an acorn, but these squirrels burn up a lot of calories running around and digging and climbing trees. In the spring, they are busy finding the buried ones as I am pretty sure their food supply in their tree of choice is running low. Sometimes people bring peanuts or sunflower seeds and scatter them around the base of the old oaks for them. I don't know if it's like hitting the motherlode for them, but I hope it is! I was surprised when I first started walking in the park at the different colors of the squirrels. I don't recall ever seeing a black one on any TV show. I thought it was an oddity at first, like a reverse albino. I discovered that there were several of them, so it's just a color. They all look the same to me. I can't tell boy from girl or old from young. I should read up on them so I can be more knowledgeable. They scurry around and make me smile at how busy they are.

I am approached by two young women pushing strollers. Both strollers hold baby boys. They are not even close in looks. One boy is about ten months old and is of mixed race. The other boy is about a year and a half old and is blond with the bluest eyes. Both women smile and say hello back to me as I meet them and say my hello. They have the strollers loaded. It's amazing what you can put in one of them. They have everything they need for a day in the park. Things the little boys will not do without as their moms have prepared for this outing. Both women are married to military men. This city has an air force base north of the park. There is a large population of active and retired military here. The air force is very much busy all the time like the squirrels, always preparing and planning for the future, never living in the moment. Military life prepares and disciplines the service men and women to be ready. Very much like the loaded strollers with needed items stocked, the busy squirrels stock their homes in the fall for the cold hard winters. I find it very amazing that there is such similarity between the little busy squirrels and the stroller-pushing moms.

The mother with the younger son has had some ups and downs in her life. She has always been a little different, but nothing really out there. Being the middle child in the family and the only girl, she had a lot of attention growing up, but was the opposite of her mom. If her mom said red, she said green. If her mom liked stripes, she liked polka dots. They got along for the most part, and her growing up in rural America made her want to explore and discover new adventures as she got older and ready to graduate. Coming from a family of modest means, she figured that a way to get to see the world would be to join the air force. She had always been a good student, and the process to enlist and get accepted went smoothly. She didn't think she would make it through basic training, but pulled up her big girl pants and stuck with it. No one was more proud than her when she completed her training. After having the good fortune of being sent to Germany to serve, she met the greatest friend and companion. She later married him in a wonderful service with family and friends. The hard part was telling her folks and breaking the news to them that she had accepted his proposal. When she mentioned that he was all the things she had ever dreamed of having in a spouse, her folks were very happy for her. The bombshell was to then mention that he was black. It's not that it makes any difference to her, but she knew that her parents were raised old-school and believed that you didn't mix the races. No matter what her parents believed or counseled her about, she knew that this guy was a keeper. She would walk in this world with him, and they would be okay.

It was difficult for a while to talk to her folks about wedding plans, but she stuck to her plan and did not let anything or anyone deter her. Once released from her military service, her civilian life as the spouse of a military man who was determined to make a career in the military was to support and love this man whom she adored. Her folks were cold at first, and the couple knew that time heals all wounds. It took several years for her dad not to look so damn sad when he saw her. Fortunately, her brothers were more open-minded and embraced her husband in friendship, and they got along very well. The nice part was not living in close proximity to any of her or his family. That blessing manifests itself in the fact that each family didn't know the day-to-day comings and goings of her life. She didn't have to let them know anything, and they didn't have to burden her with what they were doing.

They ended up moving to this city as a positive career move for her husband. There is a great group of people in the air force here, and she and her husband made friends and have a super fun social life. They started talking about a family and decided that this was a good place to start that. It didn't take very long, and she knew she was pregnant. Now the hard part was going to be telling her parents. She decided she wouldn't tell them until she absolutely had to. She very much knew how her dad felt about interracial marriage, but interracial grandchildren was a whole new territory. As much as she mulled it over in her mind and talked to her husband, she just didn't believe her dad, especially, was going to be happy. She shouldn't have let it bother her so much. As she did what she wanted to do without her parents' permission, but this was different. So she was thankful the secret was hers and she didn't live real close to family.

At the beginning of summer, her mother called, and they had a nice long conversation. Toward the end of the call, she stated that her father and she would be taking a road trip and would be coming over the Memorial Day holiday. Needless to say, controlling the panic in her voice was a real effort. Not only would she be showing, she would be less than two months from delivering. Having had no complications and feeling radiant during this whole pregnancy, this would be the first glitch.

She prepared and put everything in place for Memorial Day. She planned like a military procedure. Nothing overlooked, no surprise anything. If busy-as-the-squirrels were a way to describe her frame of mind and actions, she was a role model. As the holiday closed in, her anxiety rose.

As her husband and she greeted her parents as they walked up the walkway to her home that beautiful May day, tears flowed from her mom's eyes after the look of surprise. Her dad was somber but shook hands with her husband before he turned and looked her in the eye and said, "Girl, you really did it now." He took her gently and hugged her, but not too tight. He kissed her neck and whispered, "What am I going to do with you?"

She whispered back, "Continue to let me fly."

After good food and much talk about everything under the sun, her folks were on their way four days later.

Their son was born on a hot day about two months later. They gave him her father's first name as a middle name. Her father was proud of that and was very enamored with the little guy. He couldn't wait until the child was old enough to play catch or he could take him fishing. They would have a tight relationship. She just knew. It's amazing the love of a grandparent and grandchild. It's not as stressful as the parent-child relationships.

Today she strolls her son with her friend in the park and plans with detail the summer visit of her mom and dad, who can't get enough photos of the little guy who melted the coldness of age-long beliefs of who should marry who.

14

Repeated History

LIGHT RAIN EARLIER TODAY LEFT the park air smelling clean and refreshed. The sun is out in full by the time I start walking, and it makes for a very pleasant walk. As I come around the backside of the path, I find a turtle on the path. It's not a real large one, about the size of a grape fruit. I pick it up and am amazed at how heavy it is for its size. Turtles are some of the oldest of creatures still in our world today. They often are used to symbolize the earth with persistence and their endurance. I have never held a turtle before this and place it back into the plants and off the path. I again have seen something new on my walks in this park. I smile that maybe I saved this animal, which will probably live a hundred years.

As he approached, I felt that he was pretty sure of himself. The long strides and the confident gait made me think this. As he got close, I said hello. He said, "Hello, what a beautiful day." I agreed, and we each set off in opposite directions.

He was self-made with his business. He had changed directions with what he was doing several times. Most always the need was due to the economy and the consumers' needs. He followed a family of business owners. The previous two generations all owned mom-and-pop businesses. Mostly serving the consumer and what they could provide and make a living off of them. His parents did well for a number of years, and he grew up in those affluent times. When his folks just started out, he had heard how hard it was and how they had sacrificed for his brother and himself. He had had to work from the time he was very young in the family business, mostly stocking items when he was young and gradually learning to do other chores required to keep the business going. He never complained about helping out. He very much enjoyed the public who came in to buy supplies. In a way, he grew up in an adult world, as there was no time to play with other children, and there were few of those in his neighborhood anyway. When he was a kid, he prayed he could grow up and be tall, wealthy, and hairy. Such were the three most desirable things he could tell from observing the older men who would talk with his mom and dad. Sometimes at night when he lay in his little cot, next to his brother in the room they shared, he prayed he would meet a really nice girl, and he would move far away and have a large family, and it would be great. But most nights, he lay in his bed, and he would tremble as he heard his parents fight and his mother cry out when his dad hit her. It didn't happen all the time, but when it did, he couldn't sleep, and he felt like God wasn't hearing his prayers when he begged God to make it stop. On those nights, he talked to God and told him that he would never hit his wife, no matter what. He felt so bad in the morning after a night like that, that he couldn't look either parent in the eye. He just watched his parents get about their day, as if nothing had happened, and he couldn't understand what their relationship was based on, that they would act this way.

As years went by, the incidents became fewer, and he was able to grasp that adults sometimes let stress and jealousy boil up in them. Those blowups didn't destroy his parents' marriage. He knew he didn't want to have that in his life as a husband, however.

He grew up, went into business with his parents, and found a girl to marry who was everything he hoped for. He branched out, started another business, and worked long days with little time off. His family started to grow, and after having two sons, his wife and he had a little girl. He was very happy for many years with his perfect, busy life, and then the economy tanked in the 1980's, which affected his bottom line. He began to struggle financially. It was at this time that he began to drink on a daily basis. It wasn't what he was drinking, it was more like why he was drinking. If his mood was black, the drinking made it blacker.

His wife had demands on her with the business, children, and the uncertainty of their financial picture. She tried to talk to him about controlling the drinking, but he blew her concerns off as she didn't know what she was talking about. With things progressing with not a lot of prospects to bail them out of their financial worries, his one and only brother died from complications from untreated pneumonia. This was devastating for him and his parents. He became mad at God for taking such a great guy when there were so many horrible, worthless, unethical villains still walking around and sucking up God's clean air. He spiraled downward with madness, grief, loneliness, and despair.

One night after drinking heavily, he came home and lost control of his mind and his promise to himself that he would never hit his wife. She really had done nothing wrong. He perceived a wrong-doing and went ballistic on her. After smacking her a few times, he threw stuff and damaged some furniture. His wife was able to stay away from him after the first few smacks, but he caught her in the hall and was trying to choke her. He was stronger than her, and it was only by the grace of God that she somehow got away. He collapsed into a somewhat blacked-out condition, and she left with the children and drove to her sister's house to stay the night.

Needless to say, the next day was hell. He felt like hell, he created hell in his home, and he didn't know how in the hell he was going to fix this. For three days he was alone. His wife wouldn't talk to him, his brother was gone, and he didn't have him to talk to. He talked to God, and he remembered how he felt as a young boy and how he listened to his parents, and he was so ashamed he had done the very thing he had promised himself so very long ago that he would not do. He asked God to help him, and he prayed his wife wouldn't divorce him. His wife agreed to talk to him but had made up her mind that she wasn't going to stay with him. They sat down together, and he promised her that he would never ever touch her in anger again. He sobbed with anguish about how he had taken out on her what was churning inside him, and he was so very sorry. He asked her to reconsider and to give him a chance. He promised he would curtail the drinking and would ask for help in dealing with his grief.

His wife made the one statement that wrung in his ears, and to this day, it reminds him that he almost lost the best thing that ever happened to him—his best friend, the mother of his children, and his business partner. She said, "I will not live with a man I am afraid of." She said it wasn't fair to her to not know who would be coming in that front door, and she would not live in fear. His promise and sincerity convinced her to forgive him.

He counts his blessings every day for what he learned about himself and his wife and his life during that time. He can honestly say that he never had a relapse and has never again touched her in anger. As always, things change, and he survived the bad years and went on to have some very profitable business ventures.

He has thoughts about retiring, but just can't quite put it together in his brain to not have anything to do on any given day. He was never one for having a lot of hobbies. He never had time to start any hobby-type things when he was a teenager and young man, as he worked all the time. He mostly enjoyed being with the love of his life and playing cards. Still very active in the day-to-day of his current business, he figures he can take baby steps to free up some time to get to a place in his mind where he can retire.

So today he takes to the path in the park to breathe in some fresh air, stretch his legs, and enjoy the life he has created by hard work and God's grace to give him a second chance with the woman he loves. He knows that forgiveness had to go both ways. It's a choice he had to give himself, as his wife gave to him. He was then able to behave his way to success.

15

Found on the Road

THERE ARE A LOT OF couples out on the path this day with strollers, little kids on beginner bikes, and carrying very little ones in their arms. It's a beautiful time to be outside. I hear fast approaching footsteps behind me and slow my pace to let a woman run by as I step to the side of the path. She waves as I say hello, and she picks up her pace again and jogs on.

She noticed all the young couples with babies and children, and it brings back a lot of memories of her having a baby this time of year, and then she is further flooded with thoughts of her childhood and life. She was seven when her dad died in an industrial accident at the coal mine he worked at. She remembers him as a fun guy who would take her mother, her brother, and herself out fishing on days off and a lot in the summer. She remembers sitting in church and singing hymns next to him and how powerful his voice was as he belted out the more upbeat hymns. Those are the two main things she remembers about him.

Her mother was left a widow at a young age and had her and her brother, who was nine at the time, to raise. She got a nice settlement from the coal company, so she didn't have to go to work in the summer. She was bound and determined to keep up the family traditions and hobbies even though her husband was gone. So they went fishing a lot, and of course, they went to church. Things settled into a nice easy pattern, and the three of them enjoyed each other and this life that had become theirs.

One hot day, returning from fishing on a shortcut dirt road, her mother got a flat tire on their old truck. Her mom knew what to do; she just didn't have the strength to do it. Once her mom got the truck jacked up, she had her and her brother put rocks in front of the tires so the truck wouldn't roll. Try as she might, she could not loosen the lug nuts. The mother realized that this is one job for a man. So they said a prayer and hoped a farmer or sportsman would come down this dirt road. After forty-five minutes, a truck approached. A single fellow stopped, rolled down his window, and spoke to her mom. He laughed when her mom told him she wasn't man enough to change the tire, and he got out to help. He looked at the young girl and smiled and said that she had sunshine for hair and that he liked it. When you're a strawberry blonde, you hear the sunshine thing a lot, but not everyone says that they like it. He made her smile, and she instantly liked him. He looked at her brother and said, "Looks like you're the man here, and I'm going to need your help. If you hold the lug nuts as I take them off, I'll help you get the spare tire, and we'll get it put on." My brother felt good to be singled out to help and beamed with pride. He went right to work and got the spare on, and everything went *click, click, click*. After exchanging a little information in conversation with her mom, he gave her his number. He told her that if she ever had a problem again, he would come over to help, what with her being a widow. She said that she wanted to pay him for his help, but he wouldn't hear of it. He just told her to pass it on and help someone else. That was his motto. So they said their goodbyes, and the family loaded up to go home. Her mom looked happy on that drive, and she personally was happy he had stopped.

A few days later, her mom called him up and told him she needed some help. He was surprised to hear from her and said, "Sure, what can I do?" She told him she had a nice pot roast, mashed potatoes, and an apple pie that needed eaten and could he come help her and her kids get it eaten. He laughed a lot over that one and said yes. So she gave him their address, and her mom spiffed up the house like the pope was coming, and they had him to dinner.

Needless to say, he came over for dinner a lot. It was always fun talking to him because he was a great storyteller. Her brother and she liked him, and she knew that her mom liked him a lot as well. They went fishing with him and had picnics and went on drives in the country. Her mom and he laughed a lot. Come winter, when they were more housebound, he taught them to play cribbage. Boy, did they have a fun time playing that game. After several months, he joined them at church one Sunday. Her mom was nervous that day. Afterward, they got to go eat at a restaurant. This was a real treat for her and her brother as her mother never took them out to eat. It all was like one happy family, and they really enjoyed that meal, even if her mom could make it better. It was a treat.

You could say they dated, but they never went anywhere alone. Everything was done with the four of them. After a summer of fishing a lot and playing horseshoes and eating burned hamburgers (he wasn't much good at barbecuing), he and her mother decided to get married. At the justice of the peace office, her mother looked very pretty in a street-length light-peach dress. He wore a suit with a peach tie. She stood next to her mom and her brother next to him. The adults repeated the vows from the judge, and they were married. They all were happy. Her brother and she had a dad, and their mom had someone to love again.

Her brother and she didn't refer to him as Dad. He had been their friend long before he married their mom. She very affectionately referred to him as Daddy'O. He liked that and smiled at her every time he saw her. He called her Sunshine, and she liked that. Her brother called him Pop and never used another term to refer to him. Daddy'O called him Hook in jest, as he had had to pull a hundred hooks out of the weeds, his clothes, and some of her clothes. Her brother was always getting a hook stuck somewhere other than in a fish. Daddy'O never complained about working it out of where it was stuck. He'd get it out and then say, "Hook, let's see where you can get it stuck this time!" They all laughed a lot when they were fishing. It was a wonderful time for the kids. It was years later as she was then a mother herself and taking her boys fishing that her mother revealed that Daddy'O never liked fishing. She told her that he really never learned as a kid and just never liked it much. Since her mom and the kids loved it and wanted to fish every chance they had, he went along and enjoyed the day and never put a damper on it for any of them. When she heard that, she was so moved with respect for him. What a gentle and kind soul to put his desires on the back burner and embrace their hobby and never once let them know the truth. She very much loved him for his kindness and this one thing in particular.

One winter evening when the kids got into their teens and they were playing marathon cribbage, he told them about being married when he was real young and that he had had a son and daughter. Of course they were curious, and he said that one day a guy was walking down the street, and his wife and kids went with him and were gone forever. We laughed and pestered him for the truth. My mom knew the story and let him spin his tale. So he said, one day he was driving down this dirt road, and he couldn't believe his eyes. Here next to the road with a flat tire were his wife and his two kids he hadn't seen for six years. He couldn't believe his luck. Well, of course, we laughed and pressed him again for the truth. He did admit that when he first laid eyes on our mom, he was smitten. The truth of his first family was that his wife took off with the children aged one and two while they were going through a divorce. He tried to find them and had thrown good money at a lazy, no-effort private investigator. With not one lead and no money to hire a better private investigator, he had to accept that he would probably never see his son and daughter. Not wanting to stay in the negative, he quickly stated he found some new kids standing by the road and stopped and picked them up for his own. Her brother and she loved that. Her mom let tears slide down her face, and they all hugged, and life was good. Her mom swore that they would make the effort to find the first children. She never heard if that happened.

When she got into high school, she met a nice boy whom she liked a lot. They hung out together and shared their dreams. They got close and then affectionate and then intimate. When she knew she was pregnant and not able to hide it, she told her mom and Daddy'O. They were not very happy but showed her love and said that they would figure this out. She had been told all her life that if she ever got pregnant, she would not have an abortion, she would not be forced to marry the father, and she would have the baby and put it up for adoption. This was her family's belief, and she knew this was the way it would be. Her folks made the plans for her to go to the home for unwed mothers, and her boyfriend signed his rights away. She went to finish her pregnancy with other girls similar to her age who were in the same predicament. The last few months dragged on. The place was okay, and she was treated well, but she was miserable. On a beautiful day toward the end of spring, she knew that this was the day. She had prepared with classes and knew what to expect. She was able to tell a nurse that her time had come, and the staff took it from there. Many hours later, she was drenched in sweat and had done her work. She heard the first cry, and she cried worse than the baby. They wouldn't let her see the child, and she was not to be told what it was. They had counseled the girls on this a lot, and she was sad she would never know. When alone in a room with a kind nurse recovering from having just given birth, the nurse whispered in her ear, "Do you want to know if it was a boy or girl?" She nodded yes. The nurse said "boy" and finished her business with her and left. She was released a few days later, and her mom and Daddy'O came to drive her home for the rest of her recovery and to get her through the rest of her high school years and graduation. She cried the whole drive home. Daddy'O told her many times that she needed to remember that another person can love another's child and that she needed to believe that for closure. So she prayed that her son had a good home with loving parents.

During her senior year, she reconnected with the father of her son. They were still young but a hell of a lot wiser. Their relationship was with a common bond, and they got along well. It wasn't easy, and it wasn't hard. There were just some issues they had that were harder than others. After graduation, they moved in together and decided to marry. They then had another son. She was often told that he was a replacement for the son they gave away. She hated that. People didn't understand the hurt and anguish of their decision and that they in no way replaced their first child. They then in a few years were fortunate and had a second son. The two boys were very different from each other, and her husband and she wondered if their first son was dark like the second son and his father's family or fair like her and her family. Her husband and she had fun with the boys, with Daddy'O and her mom, and with Uncle Hook. They had the best of times fishing and playing baseball. They were all a great family, but always thought of their first son.

When the boys were old enough to understand, they told them about their older full brother. They explained that they were young and that what they chose to do at that time was best for everyone. Their sons seemed more eager to find him the older they got. So they started a search. They gave out a lot of information on websites and prayed they might get some information. Many months later, she was called by a woman who explained she was the mother of the boy they were probably looking for. She wanted them to meet her son, as he had always known he was adopted and had said that he wanted one day to find his birth parents.

Needless to say, the first son could not believe that he had two full brothers. It was beyond amazing to all of them that the first son was not a blond or a dark-haired boy, but a redhead! Daddy'O had so much fun with that when he found out. He gave her lots of ribbing about spreading her sunshine around. They cried and laughed and cried some more about the good fortune that their oldest son was raised right, had a loving family, and was a good person. Daddy'O was the proudest of them all, as he exclaimed, "How blessed we are to know what had happened to our child." He never knew anything about his first children. He would hug her and her husband and kid them about storks dropping babies off at the wrong doorsteps and how they needed to always sing "You Are My Sunshine" and thank the Lord.

So as she ran in the sunshine and these happy thoughts fill her with joy, she thought to herself that today would be a good day to go fishing. She remembers Daddy'O and the love of a man who didn't need to be what he was to her. He did what he did because he was a good Christian man who one sun-filled day found her, her mother, and her brother broke down on the side of the road.

16

Money Help

WHEN THE SUMMERTIME COMES TO the park, there is a lot going on. Families on outings fill the playground with children. Photographers use the park as a backdrop for their photo sessions. There are several photo sessions going on today. As I walk, I see one group that is definitely a wedding party getting posed for the photos. There is a small family having photos taken with the children wearing matching outfits. It reminds me of how my parents used to dress all of us kids alike. I smile at that thought.

I see a younger man jogging toward me. It is obvious that he has been doing this for a while as he is covered with sweat. He is drenched in it. I say my hello, and he waves and nods acknowledgement.

He's running physically but trying to run away in his mind. He did not know when he came to this city to go to college on a football scholarship that he would get so far in debt. It wasn't the schooling or living conditions that were draining him, it was the nightlife and his introduction to gambling. Having lived in a state that did not have gambling, coming here was a pleasant surprise to have it offered and for him to be able to participate. You don't have to go to the bars to gamble, you can buy lottery tickets at all the convenience stores. With the idea in mind of how fun it would be to win a nice jackpot, he weekly bought tickets for all the jackpots. With every bit of spare money he had, he plopped it down for that one chance to win something. He opened a few credit card accounts with the intention of using the line of credit for extra cash. He didn't realize that the cash withdrawals had a 25.1% interest rate, so it didn't take long and a few cash withdrawals and his credit limit was maxed.

He began cutting money expenses on everything he did. He ate the cheapest meals he could find. He only bought off-brands for everything he ate and for personal care items. He quit washing his clothes so often and now never washed his car. After a few months, he figured he would move into a cheaper apartment. He was thrilled when he found a one-bedroom basement apartment for $300 cheaper a month than he was now paying. The landlord/homeowner was a retired accountant and very friendly. He moved in as soon as he could. His thought of saving money on rent to pay back his credit cards went out the window when the ready cash in his hands tempted him to buy tickets to get out of debt quick if he won.

Several times he would wander outside his apartment and talk with the owner. They seemed to hit it off pretty well, and it didn't take long before he was asked by the accountant if he could help him out with his new phone. One thing led to another, and he helped him and his wife with the new computer and helped them navigate the social media sites and set up. Every time he did something for them, they wanted to pay him, and he always declined. He knew he could really use the money, but didn't reveal his financial situation to the couple. Things went well for him with his schooling and sports, and life in general, all except the amount of money he owed.

One night he was invited to dinner with his landlords, and he eagerly accepted. He hadn't had a good homemade meal in a long time, and this would be a treat. Dinner was excellent, and afterward over cake and coffee, he just blurted out to the accountant, "How do you get ahead of credit card debt?" After all, the guy was a retired accountant, so maybe he thought he had a magic plan of how to make more money. The accountant asked a few questions, and his story came pouring out. He felt so ashamed to actually say that he had gambled the money away. Showing compassion and understanding for the young man's plight, the accountant asked him to bring his bills and expenses over, and he would take a look at everything and give him his opinion. The accountant then said that the big misconnection most people have is that they need to make more money when the truth is that they need to spend the money they make more wisely.

A few days later, he took his folder over with his payments and bills and plopped it all down for the accountant. When he asked what it would cost him, the accountant smiled and told him that they would barter. Not knowing exactly what that meant, he asked again what he had to pay him for his help. The accountant said, "Look at it this way, young man. You helped me with the computer and phone. I am going to help you with a financial plan. It's the young helping the old and the old helping the young."

After reviewing all his information, the accountant had a plan in place, but knew nothing would work if the young man wouldn't follow through. So before he laid out the plan, he had a real heart-to-heart with him. He asked him how badly he wanted to get this debt paid off. He asked if he was willing to make sacrifices to get it paid off. The young man seemed sincere in his responses and generally embarrassed he was in this fix. So the accountant laid out the plan. First and most important was that the young man was going to have to be accountable to the accountant each month and bring over the new billing statements for his review. That way, any new debt would be up front, and he would have to answer for it. Second, he needed a better hobby or leisure-time activity rather than gambling. When his interests were discussed, they figured out that jogging was cheap, better for his health, and would be easy to do. This would be the hard one for him to do as he was on his own to follow through and derail his desires to gamble by jogging and walking. The third step was to apply for a zero-interest credit card, transfer the balance of the higher-rated cards, and not ever get cash off the card. Fortunately, his credit was not damaged, and he was able to do this but not pay off the other cards completely. This now was the first priority in the repayment plan, to pay off the balance on the higher-interest cards.

The budget was tight, and he had no wiggle room for gambling money. He didn't feel deprived by not gambling, but he had no social or nightlife what with staying away from temptation. He noticed that the accountant's wife invited him to dinner more often. This was really a delight to him as he wasn't much of a cook, and Top Ramen noodles could be cooked just so many ways. He knew it was a kindness that helped him out financially. She always sent him home with leftovers.

Four months later, he had the first card paid off. The accountant told him to freeze the card in a can of water, and this card would be his emergency card. He didn't want to close the card as it would hurt his credit because the line of credit available to him would be lessened and his score could go down. The accountant then had him negotiate with the credit card company to lower the interest rate, and much to his surprise, he was able to do that. So now he had the beginning of the plan in place.

When he got nervous or lonely, he would jog. At first he was mad at himself and would run in anger. Eventually he ran to help himself out. He noticed some pretty nice girls who jogged at the college track, and he would occasionally go to the park for a different scenic run.

When the second card was paid off, and he started to see the light at the end of the tunnel, he had a visit with the accountant. Being pleased with his progress, the accountant wanted to know where his head was at. After gathering that the young man was happy but not satisfied, he told him his favorite saying that he himself lived by. He said, "Son, there are two things to aim at in life: first, to get what you want and, after that, to enjoy it. Only the wisest of mankind achieve the second." This is a quote from Logan Pearsall Smith. With that he explained that now was the time for him to give himself credit for working at his goal and achieving part of it. He needed to be happy with his choice and not continue to feel disappointed in himself. Only he could give himself the freedom of accomplishment.

So he opened his eyes to a new day and thanked the Lord for putting the accountant in his life to help him find some happiness. Now he was determined to enjoy his life and continue on the right path to financial security.

As he slowly chipped away at paying off his debt, he jogged in his free time. He smiled when he opened his freezer and saw his frozen assets and had joy knowing he would never use it for a million-to-one shot at wealth.

Liquid Diet Blessing

THE PARK IS A BUSY place in the summer. With the children out of school, the park provides a place for them to play and picnic. There is a lot of activity with the farmers market that sets up for individuals to sell their products. A lot of people come to buy the healthier version of produce and naturally grown and made honey, jams, and baked goods. With the push to take artificial out of the food supply by consumer demand, these people have a steady supply of customers wanting to buy natural and organic.

I am approached by a grandmother and granddaughter who are taking a stroll after buying products from the vendors. I say hello, and the young girl says hi while the grandma talks on the phone. She is telling her daughter, the mother of the granddaughter, about the produce they bought that day and the prices for the items. In her attempt to be healthy, cook healthy, and eat healthy, she is a frequent shopper at the market.

She and her husband had made an agreement many years ago that they wanted to be in good physical shape to travel, enjoy their retirement, and to do things with their grandchildren when they got older. Having stuck to that plan most of their lives, they did alter the way they ate a few years back when both started having higher cholesterol levels. Each had their yearly checkups and had few medical issues that were not age-related.

One year, around her husband's fifty-fifth birthday, she asked him what he would like to do to celebrate. He didn't want to do anything special, and going out to dinner was decided on. She did say that she wanted to give him a special present this year. Something she had thought about for a long time and that they both would enjoy. He asked what it was, and she said, "For ease of mind and for the betterment of your health, I want you to have a colonoscopy." Needless to say, he was not impressed at her suggestion. She further explained that she had researched it and they had good medical coverage to pay for most of it. She felt the ease of mind would be a blessing. He hum-hawed around and said he couldn't stand being awake for this and that he was terrified at how much it might hurt. She laughed and explained how he would be asleep for the procedure and that the worst part would be the preparation. That was done in advance to clean everything out. She reinforced the facts that colon cancer was the silent killer and, without early detection, could be devastating. But with an examination that found no complications, the ease of mind would benefit them both. Her major concern was that he was at an age to get it done. She added that she would do the examination when she turned fifty-five. Reluctantly, he agreed. They were able to schedule the procedure to be done in four months' time.

When the time came, he complained through the entire process. She reminded him repeatedly that he promised. So after the day of the prep hell and the examination done with him feeling nothing, he got a clean bill of health. They both found joy in that and thanked God that they had done the right thing and now had ease of mind.

Several years later, as she was approaching her fifty-fifth birthday, she knew she had to honor her promise and also have the procedure. Knowing that her husband had sailed through everything without complications, she had little worries. When she set up her appointment for the procedure, she and her husband had a lot of good laughs at what a hell the prep was. Who in their right mind would ever go on a liquid diet? When she woke from the anesthesia in a hospital room, she had to take a bit to get her wits about her.

She hadn't expected this, as this was not what happened with her husband. Looking into her husband's eyes, she knew that he was troubled and had possibly been crying. Groggily she asked what had happened. He explained that they had found a cancer. It was small, and they were able to remove it as they found it in time. Everything she feared and wanted to prevent just smacked her with reality. She asked if they for sure got it all. He said the doctor was very confident that he did and that he would be back in to see her in a couple of hours.

Being reassured by the doctor and subsequent follow-up examinations over the years had her feeling very good about life and having the quality of life to enjoy her husband and their time together along with her precious granddaughter.

As she walks and talks with her granddaughter on the path, she feels well and most of all happy that she took her own advice and had the colonoscopy. She takes special care to show her love to all she has in her life because she knows how precious and uncertain our lives are. As beautiful as the park is today, she is grateful for her beautiful life.

18

Teaching Children

TODAY THERE IS A BIRTHDAY party celebration happening in one of the areas where there are a lot of picnic tables and barbecue stands. This park is set up conveniently for families, friends, and organizations to get together for outdoor picnics.

As I walk today I hear a lot of talking and noise behind me. I take a quick peek backward and realize that there is a family approaching me: a father and wife walking, and two children on Rollerblades. As we approach a fork in the path, I step to the side to let them pass. At each intersection of the park, it is posted with signage that "This is a walking trail only. No bikes, skateboards, or Rollerblades allowed." The older of the children reads the sign out loud and then turns to the dad and says, "Dad?" The father says, "It's okay, let's keep going." The kids skate by me, and the parents say "Excuse us" as I say hello. I stand in wonderment at what just happened and know that this father and mother believe all rules apply to everyone but them and are teaching their children by their bad example that it's okay for them not to go by the rules. I say to myself, "Well, hello, Mom and Dad. Just wait until the children are older. In only a few years, your lack of teaching and example setting will slap you in the face." Kids make bad choices and need the role model of law-abiding parents.

As I continue on, I meet a three-generation trio of women. It's obvious to me that it's a mother, daughter, and granddaughter who have decided to walk the path today. I say hello, and they respond with hi and smiles. Grandma has come to visit for two weeks and to spend time with her daughter and granddaughter. The granddaughter is now in her teens and has a very close bond with her grandma. The grandma lives in another state and takes the train to come visit. Many times the daughter and granddaughter ride the train to visit her. When they do, they do fun things together like shopping, gardening, canning, cooking, going to art shows, and going to music productions. The best part is just teaching the granddaughter the very same things she once taught her daughter. Her granddaughter is a lot like her and loves pretty much the same things as she does. It's funny how her granddaughter is more like her than her own daughter. They love the same colors, and when they shop together, the grandmother can always pick out clothes that the granddaughter will wear. They have a love for the same kind of music and enjoy singing songs together too. They both are interested in arts and crafts. They have fun making things out of nothing and being proud of the end result. There is always some sort of craft to make, and they enjoy creating. There are simple things too. Like doing things for other people and helping out when someone has hit hard times. Volunteering at the soup kitchen gives them this satisfaction of helping their fellow man. Selecting a family to help at Christmastime is also one of the more special things they do together. With the family in question, they shop, bake, wrap, and deliver a special gift-giving experience. This has been done since the grandmother's daughter was a little girl and will be done as long as she is alive. They enjoy going to church and singing the hymns. The grandmother taught Sunday school for over twenty years and has always been able to tell the Bible stories from heart. As a real little girl, the granddaughter loved the grandmother to tell or read the stories to her. She hopes that soon she will be able to help out at vacation Bible school as she is now getting old enough to be a helper and not a student. They planted in the garden, and the granddaughter was always eager to learn. The grandmother taught her to plant with love. As they harvest the vegetables, they then will cook the love they have grown. The grandmother teaches her granddaughter to tend the gardens as if they were her children. Always being careful and tender with the new plants and giving them room to grow—every day watching, watering, and tending the plants. Just like children, weeding out the bad that want to crowd in and get a foothold in their life, being watchful for sickness and the need for plan B if something goes wrong. It is always a special time to harvest and to start canning as each of them has their special jobs. The end results are a lot of satisfaction that what they have done is done with love because they planted love.

She teaches her granddaughter to follow step-by-step instructions with baking and cooking. It's kind of a "follow the rules or you won't get a good result." As with raising kids or making a cake or pickling beets, the same rules apply. She is proud that this lesson is learned by her granddaughter and that her daughter is raising a lovely girl.

As they stroll on the path and make plans for the next few days, they enjoy each other and the gift they are to each other, taking special time to nurture and care for their relationships. The grandmother knows that her beautiful daughter and granddaughter have beauty on the inside as well as the outside. So they will finish their walk, have a nice lunch, weed the flower beds, and watch a favorite movie in the evening after cooking with love and as they use the homemade spaghetti sauce they canned last fall.

19

Bread of Life

TODAY, WALKING IN THE PARK is a beehive of activity. Children are out of school, and the playground and water park are full of parents, caretakers, grandparents, children, babies, and preteens. Only a few take to the walking path as most just want to enjoy the playground.

I am approached by a woman who is enjoying a stroll today as her two boys play at the water park with her father-in-law, who is monitoring them while she takes a short stroll. I pass and say hello. She responds happily with a "Have a good day." Her father-in-law came to live with her, her husband, and her two boys several years ago. He had been retired from teaching history and had been living on his own after his wife's death. Her husband had asked her one day if they could sell their home and buy a larger one so that his dad could live with them. She had always gotten along with him and considered him quite the character. The first time she met him, he winked at her and said his son had done well.

When they approached her father-in-law about changing his living arrangements, he had some concerns and questions, but then agreed to move with them if three things that he requested were met. He asked that he have a room with space enough for his books. He was very attached to his reading material. He wanted to continue to learn always so he could be, as he said, "an educated tourist" as he got older. This he said with a wink of his eye and a little laugh. His second request was that they pray before every meal. The third was that they have bread at every meal.

Her husband and she were eager to meet these requirements as all three would be easy to accomplish. They already prayed before the evening meal, so implementing a prayer before breakfast and lunch was not a problem. She was a fine baker and actually enjoyed baking bread. Serving it at all meals in one form or another would not be a challenge at all.

They all went house hunting together and were able to find a very nice place with mother-in-law quarters. With a little carpentry work, shelves were installed on one whole wall in his living room space. He would get his own privacy and the library wall of books he needed to meet the #1 request he had. Once the final arrangements were made and they all relocated, they settled into a very comfortable life.

Every day at 11:00 a.m. he would come into the main house and open a beer and pour half in one glass and half in another glass. He would then ask her to join him, and they would toast the good Lord to watch over his wife until he could join her and sit and sip the beer. On the weekends, her husband enjoyed this ritual with his dad. They would talk about the local news, sports, the government and politics, religion, signs of the times, his job, health issues, and it was nice. During the week, she had the privilege of the 11:00 a.m. ritual. Not being a beer drinker, she asked if she could add tomato or Clamato juice to help her swallow the beer. He had no problem with that and would set out the juice on the weekdays when she would join him. They would talk, and he would tell her many interesting stories about his parents, his childhood and teenage years. He would talk about his young married life, his teaching career, her husband's childhood, and, of course, the history of the world.

He would watch her as she did her cooking and baking and was just like a kid in a candy store when she pulled hot rolls, bread, cookies, or pie from the oven. He would be so eager to have a nice slice of warm bread he would slather with butter and thank God for the bread of life. She noticed that before he ever took his first bite of bread or a roll, he would put it to his lips, give it a kiss, and then silently thank God; and then he would eat.

Watching her make a pie one day, he told her that he only liked two kinds of pie. Not knowing this before, she was quite interested that he hadn't said anything before. She said she sure hoped the apple pie she was making was one of them! He winked and smiled at her and told her he only liked hot and cold. She laughed with him over that one. They shared a lot of pie after that as she made sure she made pie every week, sometimes two different kinds on the same day.

He had one job, and he was dedicated to this job he picked for himself to do. Every day he would stand at the front window and wait for the school bus to drive past the house to the bus stop. On cold days, he waited inside the front door for the boys to open the door and come in. On warm days, he would wait on the porch for them to come up the sidewalk and climb up the steps. Every day he would rough up their hair and say, "Welcome home, my boys!" He hugged them and would usher them in the house and to the kitchen, where he was totally in charge of getting them their after-school snack. He would set out a glass of milk or cold lemonade, and on cold days, a mug of cocoa. He would then put out cookies, cake, pie, or sliced bread covered with apple butter or peanut butter and jam. The boys had to wait to eat until he said grace, and they would then scarf up this belly-filling afternoon snack. He would drink a cup of coffee and ask them what they learned at school. At first, the boys would say "nothing." He would not hear of it! He said to them that they had been gone for eight hours and they had to have learned something that day. He said he would not let them leave the table until they told him something they had learned. This meant that their chores, homework, or playtime would have to wait until they could tell him something they had learned.

The boys were quick studies and soon learned that they could tell him not only something learned in class, but something from the playground or from looking out the bus window. Each day they would sit, enjoy talking about their day, and eat the snack he placed in front of them. The mom would let the grandpa have his time with the boys, and she would thumb through a magazine in the living room and listen to their conversations.

One day while making pie, she asked him if he truly did have a favorite pie. He said it had been many years since he had it, but his grandma, mother, and then his wife had all been able to make concord grape pie. He said it was his all-time favorite and it brought back many wonderful memories for him. She told him that she had never heard of it. He told her that it was probably in the old cookbook his wife had used most of their married life. He then got up and went to his living quarters and, not too long after, returned with a leather-bound book that had been well used. He gave it to her and said that he would be pleased if she would take it. He wanted her to have it. She thumbed through the pages with so many clippings, handwritten notes, and recipes until she found the pie recipe. After studying it, she realized that there were several steps to prepare the fruit filling, but the pie was quite simple. Not knowing if she could buy concord grapes, she made it her mission to look for them every time she went grocery shopping. One summer day, she hit pay dirt. While picking out melons and bananas, she saw that the grapes were there. She was very excited and knew she was going to surprise her father-in-law with his first concord grape pie in years.

She was never so nervous making a pie as she was this one. She did not want to mess it up. So she followed the steps written by her mother-in-law and carefully put it all together and popped it in the oven. It smelled wonderful baking, and she had a constant smile on her face. When her father-in-law came in to have lunch, he had a twinkle in his eye that she noticed. He ate his soup and bread and then asked what they were having for dessert. She tried to play coy, but he had known since he smelled it baking. She was very proud to place the pie in front of him. He let tears fall and told her that this was the best treat ever and he loved her for making it for him. He served it up on two plates, and they savored each bite as if it were heaven. Never before had she enjoyed a piece of pie as she did that day. It wasn't the pie so much as it was the moment shared with him. It made a special bond for the two of them.

When he first came to live with them, and he would do his afternoon after-school snack with the boys, the boys would tear off some of the outer crust of their bread and place it on the plate. He would tell them they needed to eat it, and they would say they didn't like the crust so much. He then told them the story of the hard bread crust and how nutritious it is and how they should always eat it. His mother had told him that during the war, many people were rounded up and sent to the concentration camp prisons. The food was terrible and very meager. Many people were there and many were sick. On a daily basis they got a bowl of thin broth and a chunk of bread. Sometimes the bread was quite hard and very hard to chew. Often the very sick people would trade their hard crusty bread for the thin broth as the warm broth felt good on their sore throats and warned them up temporarily. So many of them died, and the broth never helped them get better.

At the end of the war, many doctors were amazed at how healthy some prisoners were and that so many others were so very starved. It was discovered that the prisoners who traded the thin broth for the hard crusty bread were the ones who were in better shape.

He then told the boys that chewing the crust was maybe not what they liked to eat, but that it was the bread of life they needed to grow strong and healthy. So the boys always ate the crusts after that.

One of the nice things for her was that at the farmers market or the local grocery stores there was always a nice variety of lovely breads to pick up if she didn't feel like making homemade. Today, though, she had gotten up and started a batch of bread. She now needed to finish her walk, gather up her boys and her father-in-law, and go home to knead and shape some loaves. She is thankful she gets to break bread with a wonderful man she married and his wise and witty father, who has blessed their lives with abundance and happiness.

20

Special Calling

THE MOWERS ARE OUT MOWING today. The smell of fresh-cut grass is a wonderful smell of summer. It makes me sneeze sometimes, but it is only a temporary reaction to such a memory-reminding smell.

I am reminded of mowing grass as a child with the push lawn mower we had. I liked doing it as the lawn looked tidy and neat when first done. I made a special effort to make straight rows as I mowed so I didn't miss any grass that needed cut. The hard part of a push mower is going uphill. If the grass is long, it's a real workout.

I am approached by a caretaker pushing a disabled young man in a wheelchair. There is another special child with Down's syndrome walking behind them with her caretaker. I say hello, and the caretakers say hi, but the young man and woman do not. The nature walk they are on has the young girl collecting bird feathers or flowers that are blooming.

I have been pleasantly surprised to see dame's rocket flowers blooming along the river channel banks. I am sure the seeds blew in long ago with a high wind and established themselves. They're a bit out of place with the thistles and other weeds, but a lovely flower to see nonetheless.

One of the caretakers has not worked with the special needs children and teenagers for very long. She didn't really know she could do this line of work to help the less fortunate, but has now found it to be her calling.

Her parents divorced when she was young, and she lived during the school year with her mom. Summertime had her and her brother going to stay with her father, who lived several states away. Her mother did not do really well with the divorce and took to drinking a lot. She would stay up in the evenings and play cards with her mother while her mother drank. Not having any social life, her mother stayed at home and waited until evening to play cards with her and tell her stories. Over the course of time, her mother told her many things she did not want to know. She would listen and let her mom vent. There was nothing good said about her father and his new wife. She soon learned that the card-playing sessions were her mother's way of expressing her anger at what her life had become.

When she graduated from high school, she found employment serving the public. Once she was old enough, she started tending bar. Again, she became a listener. People of all walks of life would talk to her, and she would listen to their stories. Her input wasn't really wanted, the patrons just wanted to vent. Quite often she would hear things she really didn't want to know. She, however, never repeated anything she heard and tried very hard to be as nice as possible to those who had sadness and hate in their lives. She was considerate to all she waited on and created a following of sorts with the clientele. She noticed over the years that most people wanted to talk about negative or sad things in their lives. As happy and joyful as she greeted them, the conversation most often turned to some sort of bad event or situation that the customer wanted to vent about.

Feeling a bit stagnant with her job after years of bartending, she wondered if a career change would be worth it. While she researched job opportunities, she read about the field of helping with the special needs children and teenagers. They were requesting compassionate caretakers who had people skills. She felt that she at least had that, so she applied and was called in for an interview.

Not knowing if she really was going to do this line of work, she had the opportunity to shadow the care workers for one week. The experience was eye-opening to her. Everyone involved with the handicapped had such positive attitudes. The families were amazing people who felt so blessed to have their special needs child in their lives. Every step in the child's learning advancement was celebrated with happiness, and most of all the children were happy. They didn't seem to have any worries. It was refreshing to be around such a positive environment.

She decided to work with the children and found a calling she didn't know she had. One thought that she soon believed was that God doesn't make any mistakes, and anyone who looks down on the less fortunate has issues that they need to deal with. The families of these children feel more blessed than disappointed by their handicapped child. One mother told her that the children were special flowers in the garden of life. She was also told that the caretakers were special blessings to the families and, most of all, the children.

She learned to take baby steps with teaching her special wards. Very much like pushing a lawn mower uphill. It's a lot harder and slower, but it can be done. The results are a sense of satisfaction to everyone involved with the process.

Today, walking on the nature walk as she pushes her special guy along, she knows that God made us all different for a reason. She is very glad that she found the reason for her to involve her life with the special flowers of God's creation. She would never stop listening to the pride the parents and teachers have for accomplishments made by those she now would always work with.

21

Grasshopper Mentor

WALKING TODAY, I SPY A few grasshoppers on the path. They bounce away as soon as you get close. I feel that they must sense the vibration of my footsteps on the path surface. Grasshoppers can only move forward. They can easily get carried by the wind, and there are many varieties of them.

Coming toward me is a man about my age and a young boy about seven years old. The man is pointing out the grasshoppers to the boy, and I overhear him say, "In the movie *Karate Kid*, the older Asian teacher refers to the young student as Grasshopper." He reminds the young student to have patience. He says, "Patience, young grasshopper."

I smile at the memory and say hello as I walk by. The man tells the boy to say hello to the lady. The boy shyly or reluctantly says hi. The man says to the boy that it is the right thing to do, to say hello to someone like myself. He also says hello as I pass by.

A program for older members of the community to mentor young troubled boys and girls who are in the special care of the state is very active in this city. The man decided after retiring from the railroad that he would take a hand in mentoring a young boy.

He had been an engineer for forty years with the railroad. He very much loved his job and the life he lived working for the railroad. Not ever marrying or having children, his job was his life. He very much enjoyed traveling by rail and started out as a young boy loving to travel by rail. Years ago when he was young, he and his brother would hitch a ride, so to speak, in a railcar. There was not the security there is nowadays. It was easy to do, and they had fun traveling to the next town and other states.

His mother and dad didn't worry about them, and he and his brother were gone almost all summer traveling around this way. He grew up streetwise as some older people who rode the rails taught him and his brother some tricks of the trade. These hobos, as most people referred to them, were a special family of sorts. They helped each other and passed information to each other of people, places, and things to avoid and also where there was work and food. The only time he and his brother knew they had made a mistake was when they didn't have winter coats and almost froze to death when a cold front came in and they were stranded on a train in a very cold place.

Even while he was working for the railroad, he would watch for the men and women who would travel the rails. It became somewhat a thing of the past as tighter security prevented people from getting into the cars. After he retired, he would visit cities and towns he always wanted to stop and visit. Not doing any tourist-type traveling when he was working, he thought he would enjoy it. He however found that it isn't a whole lot of fun to do by yourself. Not having his brother anymore and no family to share adventures with, he quit traveling. He filled his hours with watching hunting and fishing shows. He would go to a local pub and have a few beers and pizza on Fridays and occasionally went to church. It was with this unchanging lifestyle that he decided he would check out the caring seniors mentoring opportunity.

When he first interviewed with the child specialist, he didn't believe he had a lot to offer, but after he revealed his story of life and his work history, he was told that he would be very good as a mentor. He chose a young boy who had had a real tough go of it with his parents. He studied up on him and decided that doing some basic things with the boy at first would start a good friendship possibility.

He was warned that the young boy had a problem with lying. They had worked a lot with the boy to help him stop it, but had struggled to have total success. Knowing this, the man was not deterred and set up a movie date with the boy. He introduced himself to the young man and exchanged names and had a little light conversation before the movie. The movie was a kid's movie, not so much to the man's liking, but he was doing this for the boy. After getting soda, popcorn, and some candy, he was amazed at how much it all cost. No wonder going to the theater was a big treat.

The boy didn't talk much and only gave one-word answers when the man asked questions. Breaking the ice might take a while, and he would be patient. All in all, the first visit went well, and the boy agreed that he would like to go to the movie the next week.

Before the next visit, the man got to the home early and asked about the boy's schoolwork. Being shown the boy's folder, he realized that the boy was struggling with schoolwork. He knew he could help him, he just needed to build a trust up with the boy. When he had picked up the boy and was on the way to the movie, he asked him how his schoolwork was. The boy said "Fine." He then asked him what grade he got on his weekly spelling test. The boy said "an A." The man had seen the grade of D on the paper in the folder and knew he had lied.

He then told the boy that he had a plan for him. Each week that they would meet and do some activity, he would let the boy get three things: something to wear, something to read, and something to give to someone else. He then said, "But I will only do this if I do not catch you in a lie. Every time you lie, I will take one of the items away that you could buy. So if you lie one time, I will take the 'something to wear' away, the second lie takes the 'something to read' purchase away, and likewise for the third."

He explained that it was three strikes and you're out. No do overs and no excuses. The truth was the most important thing a person can speak. He explained that a person is known for their words and actions. Lying was not what he would want to be known for, and he was going to help him stop that habit. He explained that when the boy was going to answer a question that he might lie about, he needed to take a breath in, close his eyes, and think about the answer before opening his mouth. The man explained that he would patiently wait for an answer if the boy took his time to tell the truth.

At first, the boy just wanted to go buy three items and didn't know that he had to spend the several hours in conversation with the man first. This part was where the lies might come in. So he was disappointed this first week, as he lied about a few more things and did not get to buy anything. The following weeks had him improving and trying real hard to be truthful. He was able to pick out the "something to give someone" most often. He would choose candy for his friends or flowers for his teacher. He had lifted spirits when he returned to the home and he had something for someone.

The first time he got to get all three items, he was a very happy boy. The man was just as happy. The boy was able to get his favorite team jersey, and he was so very proud. On future weekly visits, he would wear the jersey and had a sense of fitting in where he hadn't felt like that before.

One week, after going to watch some speed racing trials at the speedway, he asked the gentleman a question. He asked if he would let him buy a jersey for his two best friends in the home. He wanted them to have one like his so they would all look the same. When asked why this was important, he replied because he wanted to do something nice for his friends as no one buys them anything like this. So with careful consideration, the man said, "Well, I think that two jerseys would fulfill two of the purchase requirements: one for something to wear and one for something to give someone else." The boy was on cloud nine and hugged the man for the first time.

Their friendship continued throughout the summer. It wasn't known who looked forward to the weekly visits more, the boy or the man. When they would look for an item to read, the man would guide the boy into the educational materials. He then would sit with him, and they would work out the problems or words and reading parts together. The one-on-one help had the young boy doing better with his schoolwork, and his grades were improving.

There was now happiness in the boy, which had not been in his life before. It was a patient work in progress that the man was instrumental in achieving with the young boy.

Today in the park they walk together with friendship. When the train whistle blows in the distance, the man is remembering his love of trains and starts telling the boy another story of his life, which the young man listens to eagerly as he likes this man who is patient and kind to him. As they continue on the walk, they see more grasshoppers, and the boy says, "The story you told me is kind of like us."

"In what way do you mean?" the old man says, as he gives the young man a wink.

The boy says, "You teach me like the old guy teaches the boy in the story."

The older man smiles and says, "Yes, young grasshopper, just like us."

22

Proper Life

ALONG THE WALKING TRAIL ARE sitting benches. Most all are placed along the path at a point where a person might like to take a comfortable rest. Most all have dedication plaques on them in memory of some fine family member. Things like "Take your time to enjoy God's world." "Keep smiling and walking." "Don't say you can't, you can."

I enjoy thinking about how so many do not take the time to enjoy the beauty that's right in front of them. This is a very beautiful park.

I round the corner on the trail and see a woman with her elderly mother. The mother has a walker, and they have been slowly walking from bench to bench to build up some strength in the older woman's legs. Recovering from a broken hip, she has now moved in with her daughter.

I say hello as I pass, and they both say hello back. I say that it's a lovely spot for a rest, and the mother responds that she has been doing more resting than walking. I notice the English accent. I tell her that there are no time limits on this walking path and that she should just take her time. She said she very much will, and we say goodbye.

The older woman met her American husband when he was stationed in England during his years in the service. They met at a Friday night social dance event that was a regular meeting of the young military men and the local girls. She had been attending with girlfriends for quite a while. The service men were all on their best behavior, but she was not overly interested in any of them until the time she met her future husband. He stood out to her because he didn't stand out. He was a quiet, reserved, and easygoing type. He wasn't pushy or forward. She first noticed that he wasn't smoking cigarettes like the other servicemen. He was slowly dragging on a pipe. She had always loved the smell of a pipe as her father and grandfather had smoked their pipes after the evening meal each evening. It's a habit of relaxation and seemed to be so much enjoyed by the men.

Watching this young, tall, lanky fellow, she pulled her nerve from somewhere she didn't know where and approached. He saw her coming and pulled the pipe from his mouth and cupped it in his hand. He then bent down to greet her with a very warm "you look lovely, madam, and may I introduce myself to you" kind of way. She nodded yes, and she was properly introduced to him. She said she had noticed he was smoking a pipe. He said yes, but if it offended her, he would put it away. She said she very much loved a pipe and that is why she walked over. He replied that he enjoyed his pipe. He then said again that she looked lovely and would she like to dance or sit and talk. She would have loved to dance, but her borrowed shoes were killing her feet. She didn't want to tell him that, so she suggested talking. He was greatly relieved that she didn't want to dance as he couldn't dance a step without looking like a fool. They found a window seat to sit down. They talked for hours. They talked until it was time to leave, and they made plans to meet again the next week.

Every week they discovered more and more about each other. He loved her prim-and-proper personality and the petite little thing she was. He liked that she had a bit of a sarcastic humor and that she smelled just wonderful. She liked his slow easy manner and his good looks. She liked his eyes and the way they looked at her and his big strong hands that held her and made her feel safe.

They fell in love during those Friday night get-togethers. When he knew he was going back stateside and then would be released from the service, she cried that he would be going. He told her he would send her the money to come to the States and they would marry. He gave her a cheap little gold band ring as an engagement ring and half of the airfare money before he left. When she received the balance of the money, she left England behind and joined him for her life in America. They married with the military chaplain, with his dad and brother as witnesses. His dad paid the chaplain $10 for his service. She asked the chaplain how to apply for citizenship, and the newlyweds went on a cross-country trip with a mini camper so that he could show her the places and sights of her new country. They returned after two weeks as happy as any newlyweds could be.

They moved in with his parents until they could get a place of their own. He went to work driving freight across country. He worked driving trucks all their married life, until he retired.

When they were a young couple, they had a chance to buy a fixer-upper house. It needed a lot of work, but it had great potential. She was very conservative with the household budget and would save every extra penny she could so they had money for supplies. She wanted a proper home with a formal dining room. She intended to keep her family traditions of having family meals in a lovely setting.

When he would get home after being on the road for days at a time, they always had a semi-reunion. They were very happy with each other. Each night, after a proper dinner, they would sit on the couch; he smoked his pipe, and she would knit or crochet, and they would listen to the radio. It was a comfortable fit. They always listened to the Grand Ole Opry on the radio on Friday nights. It brought them so many memories of their first Friday nights together, sitting and talking and listening to the music.

They worked on their house and spent several years getting the house up to the standards of how they wanted to live. The first thing out of the house was the carpet. She said she disliked the American like of carpeting. She loved her hardwood floors. She kept them gleaming. She kept a tidy, neat home. Everything was clean and in good order. She set a proper table. They dined with tablecloth, linen napkins, and candles.

After several years, they filled the house with children: one boy and three girls. Two of the girls were fraternal twins. One of the girls was small and petite like her, and the other was long and lanky like the dad. She very much enjoyed motherhood.

Each evening, whether her husband was home or not, she would knit, sometimes crochet, and she could embroider. She mostly knit. She knit sweaters, vests, dickies, stocking caps, scarves, and mittens and slippers for the children. She knit dresses and skirts for herself and sweaters and vests for her husband. She was extremely talented at knitting. Her end results were as pretty on the inside as they were pretty on the outside. She taught herself to knit backward so she could teach others to knit with her sitting in front of them. She would get orders to make sweaters from those who saw her handiwork and would pay her. She often had people in her beautiful tidy home for measurements. Many items she made she sold at a local woman's shop. She had special labels made and sewn into the clothing that the item was handmade by her. This shop sent many women her way to order sweaters. She would help them pour over catalogues to find the perfect style. Picking the yarn was up to them. She would figure out in the instructions what was needed, and they would buy the skeins of yarn and bring them to her. She was sometimes surprised at the color yarn someone would pick. She never made anything that wasn't lovely.

One day she was outside doing some weeding in the garden when a young man selling high-end vacuums and working the block asked if he could demonstrate the vacuum for her, and if she did, he would give her a case of soup. Being very conservative with money and always in need of something she could use that didn't cost anything, she said yes. She then asked him if it was for sure that she would get a case of soup if she watched his demonstration. He declared yes, and she led him up the porch and opened the front door into the front room with the most beautiful high-glossed wooden floors he'd ever seen. The floor glowed with shininess. She said the look of horror on his face was priceless. He stammered and stuttered and asked if he could call his boss. She led him to the kitchen wall phone. He quickly told his boss that after promising this lady a case of soup, he found out that she had no carpeting and asked what he should do. The boss told him to demonstrate the vacuum and give her the case of soup.

The young man did his best to demonstrate the vacuum, and when he was done, he asked with a sales pitch if she would like to buy a vacuum on a payment plan, just in case she would put carpet down. She looked at him squarely and asked, "Why would I ever cover up my beautiful floors with carpet?" He agreed that that would be a shame. He went and got her the case of soup, and she thanked him. She laughed and laughed over the years as people would comment on her pretty floors. She would tell the story, and everyone would laugh.

The children were raised with manners—to be respectable and to honor their elders. They had family meals together on the good dishes. She wasn't saving the good dishes for company or for holidays when every day her family was the best company. They had to change into clean clothes to eat as playclothes were not proper attire. Her husband would even put a tie on to please her.

When her husband retired from driving the roads of the nation, they wanted to travel to places she had not seen. They were able to make many trips and see most of the 417 national parks the United States has. After a few years, their very comfortable life saw them each experiencing some medical issues.

When her husband was diagnosed with prostate cancer, he took it on, in his slow easy way. The doctor told him he could remove the cancer and he would have four years or longer to live; and if he didn't remove it, he would live four months. The couple discussed the procedure and decided he would have the surgery as they still had places to go.

The surgery went well, but no one was prepared for the blood clot that broke and ended his life. It was unexpected, and his wife was crushed as she had loved him so dearly. With her children at her side, she buried him with his beloved pipe and a promise from her that she would see him again.

She did well living on her own. She kept up her knitting as now she had grandkids to knit for, and she started knitting dog sweaters. She liked being alone and listening to the old Western songs while she knit, read, put together puzzles, and thought about her tall, lanky guy with beautiful eyes that she loved.

One night, in a bit of a hurry to close a window after the wind had picked up and was blowing the curtains into the room, she slipped on her ever gleaming slick wood floor. When she fell, she knew she broke her hip, as she heard the snap. Unable to get up or move into the kitchen to the phone, she lay on the floor all night. She was very cold, and the pain kept her up most of the night. When her daughter was unable to contact her mom the next day by phone, she decided to go check on her. After letting herself in, she found her mother, and she called 9-1-1.

Her recovery has been a series of slow steps. After the hospital, she was put into recovery care for rehabilitation. After several months there, she was released to stay with her daughter. Her daughter intends to keep her mom comfortable, happy, and well-fed for the rest of her life. She has her hands full with her mother not liking to be out of her own home. Most days her mom stares out the window, drinks her tea, and does a little handwork. She hasn't the drive to knit as she used to, but still enjoys designing sweater patterns. Her ability to do this is a testament to her extraordinary talent.

Walking in the park and resting on the benches is enjoyable for the frail English proper lady. She has enjoyed living her comfortable life in this country, not of her birth, but the country of the love of her life. The long haul road driver with the pipe in his mouth and his eyes that made her feel so very special is waiting for her. She will be patient and wait until it's time to go on that trip.

23

Not Ready Yet

TODAY THERE ARE TURKEYS IN the park. It's great to see the wild turkeys as they hang out in the city and surrounding areas. As with the
geese, they are interesting to watch and do not seem to be afraid of
the humans watching them or the traffic.

I say hello to a couple who is standing on the path observing
the turkeys, and they say hello back. We engage in a bit of conversation about the turkeys, and neither of us know if these birds taste
anything like the turkeys we get from the store. We wish each other
a good day and head out in different directions.

They have been walking engaged in heavy conversation about
family matters. Having been married for half a decade, they have gone
through some things together. There is a current problem with their
daughter's husband, who has brought tension into the family. He is
a braggart and very abrasive to them. It's something that really seems
to be getting worse. They have always wondered how their daughter
could tolerate this man, but she never complains. They know he is a
good provider to her and their three children. He has a good job, and
they have a nice home. It's just that you can't engage him in conversation about any subject. He levels. He either has to top you in your
story or cut you down to make himself seem superior. It wears a person down, and the couple doesn't want to interact with him much.
This is the problem they face. Having had family difficulties with
her brothers and their wives with the settling of her parents' estate,

she just doesn't have the energy to have discord in her life again. She thinks about how hurt she still is about the way her two older brothers and their wives treated her and her twin younger brothers, and her blood still boils. Being the only girl, she was close to her mom. It makes sense that they would be as her mom had a lot to teach her about marriage, housekeeping, maternity, and motherhood.

When her mother got older and was living alone, she and her husband were the ones to help out and visit. They cared for her yard, vehicle, and home-maintaining and repairing things. They didn't mind doing so as it was easy for her because she did not work and her husband got along with her mom really well. Her younger twin brothers would drop by and visit, but the older two brothers not so much. Her mother didn't seem to worry that she hardly saw the oldest boys. She really only felt bad when they didn't come for the holiday meals they were all to come for. Her mother, not being a selfish person, just asked the five families to be fair, which meant that if you didn't come for Christmas, then it would be fair for you to come for Easter. Time and time again the two older sons had to attend their wives' family gatherings and made no effort to be fair. Her mother was patient and would tell her, "When you have a daughter, you have her for life. When you have a son, you only have him until he takes a wife."

Sad but true. She accepted what was dealt. Her mother had been thoughtful in taking care of her final arrangements upon her death and had not treated any of the daughters-in-law or sons unfairly. Her oldest brother was named as executor because he was the oldest. She herself had made the great effort to befriend her sisters-in-law from the very start of meeting them. The two older brothers' wives gave little back in friendship, and it wasn't long before she realized they had nothing in common. The only connection she had with them was her brothers. They had little to do with her and her husband as the years went by, and she did find friendship with the twin brothers' wives. They were kind to her and her mother.

She was thankful that her best friend was her husband and that the two of them were partners in life. As her mother aged and she herself got older, she became very sentimental about her parents' things. As she dusted and cleaned her mother's house, she felt very possessive of the household items and took care to be careful with every item as she knew the day would come when everything in the house would be divided five ways, as per her mom's wishes. The day eventually came when they had to hospitalize her mom after she fell and broke her back. She never did well after that. Her daily visits to her mom allowed her to watch her mom slowly fade away. The day came when she did not wake up. She felt tremendous loss and sadness that only she, her husband, and her children experienced. Her older brothers never asked about her and made no effort of compassion to her, the only daughter.

The twin brothers' wives were very thoughtful of her. She stood in the background and let the two oldest sons take charge of all the funeral details. The funeral was nice, but the arrangement on the casket would not have been to her mother's liking at all. If she had only been asked, she would have told the oldest brother that their mother loved yellow roses, not red ones, and that her mother always felt red was too bold and too fancy for her taste. So with about ten dozen red roses sprayed all over the coffin, she again felt sad that her oldest brother didn't really know their mom or didn't care and let his wife make the selection. Her sister-in-law was always a little too fancy for her taste, and she felt that she was never good enough for the likes of her. She felt terrible that they never consulted with her about this.

She was contacted by phone that the siblings would meet at the mother's house the following Friday to start the division of personal items her folks had. The house would be sold and the proceeds divided by the five children. Any items not taken by the five would be sold or donated. She knew that this would be difficult for her. She also felt a special closeness to the items she knew that she would select, as she had a few in mind that she really wanted.

When Friday arrived and she and her husband arrived at her mom's house, her twin brothers and their wives were already there. Neither of her older brothers or their wives were there. When she entered the house, she immediately knew that things were not right. It was very obvious to everyone there that everything of value was gone. It was more than disheartening to know that the older brothers and wives had come earlier and taken items and had not honored her mother's wishes to divide the items of the parents' life fairly. As they walked through each room and reviewed the whole house and garage, they all came to the same conclusion. This was wrong. One of the twins called the oldest brother and said he, his twin, and his sister were all at the house and where were the rest of the family? He was told that he and the other brother had a scheduling conflict, so they came in early and picked a few items. Not wanting to argue about fairness, he said okay and what else did the two older brothers want? He was told that they got what they wanted and the remaining three could divide what was left. He hung up the phone, shook his head, and relayed the message to the others.

It was like a form of shock. She could not believe that she as the only daughter did not get first choice of her mother's jewelry or private sentimental items. She went from shock to sadness to anger very quickly. Everyone there felt violated to some degree.

They decided to take a few things. None of them had any joy while looking through what was the remains of their parents' lives. One brother asked if he could have his dad's old fishing pole and reel. They all told him to take anything related to fishing he could find. The other twin asked if he could have shop tools as they were full of memories for him with the projects he and his dad had worked on. The wives asked for things that were kitchen related like a set of embroidered dish towels, platters, and a teapot with a chip on the spout.

She couldn't believe that the lives of her parents were here on display to be separated and disbursed, never to have the same sentimental attachment again. So with a heavy heart, she selected a broken broach out of the few remaining items in the jewelry box, a photo in a frame of the whole family on vacation in California at the Redwoods National Park, and a few of her mother's handmade sweaters. She insisted that her sisters-in-law take items for their children. Things like the handmade sweaters and embroidered pillowcases were snatched up.

There remained a houseful of items that no one wanted and didn't have the heart to take. She wrote on a pad of paper on the kitchen counter, "You took the best, now have the rest."

They all said goodbye, kissed, hugged, and took one last look around. They shut the door on the home that was theirs for their raising and the symbol of the life their parents had made for themselves. In due course, the household items were sold, donated, or discarded. The two older brothers were only involved in this. Communications were sent by mail that the house was being marketed by a local realtor. After about a year, the final settlements were disbursed to her and her twin brothers with an itemized listing of the expenses the estate had incurred. She again was angered at the amount of money the older brother paid himself for handling the estate. She couldn't believe that she had the same blood as him. He was so greedy, selfish, and uncaring; and she had no plans of speaking to him ever again. Her younger brothers also isolated themselves from him and the second oldest brother.

With the share she received, she and her husband decided to put the money into CDs for their kids and their grandkids. They discussed their own estate plans and swore that they would not have anything like this happen to their kids. With this thought in mind, they talked a lot about the very difficult son-in-law. They really didn't want him to be the discord in their own family.

As they walked this day, they talked about how to avoid a disaster in their own lives. They were reminded of memories that still burned their eyes with hurt. She told her husband, "You know I know that when you are wronged, you are supposed to forgive as this is divine. I know that the first to forget is the better person, but I am just not ready yet." He nodded in understanding, grabbed her hand, and said, "Don't dwell on it this fine day. Walk it off."

So they walked.

24

Four Sisters

It's a fantastic day to be alive. The weather is beautiful, and the joy of being out in it is a blessing. I am walking and seeing the families of geese. Most all the eggs have hatched at this point. There are older goslings, almost as big as the parents, and there are the younger hatches. The little ones are so cute. They sure grow up fast however. Sometimes the families get all mixed up. With so many geese in the park, they gather close together in a huge herd sometimes. When they decide to go their own way, the wrong goslings go with the wrong parents. It is very funny to see a pair of geese with three large babies and two little, tiny ones. I have seen one real aggressive male take charge of thirty-five little ones that he and his life mate squire around just proud as can be. The variety of sizes of the goslings makes me laugh.

There is a lot of watching of the geese when the babies are so mobile. I walk up to a group of people taking pictures and feeding them bread. They are not supposed to feed the geese. I say hello and head out on my walk. I hear steps behind me and turn to see what I know are two sisters walking together. They look so much alike; however, one is a lot heavier than the other. I say hello and let them pass. They say hello back and continue their conversation.

The two sisters have the tightest of bonds. They both have been through hell and back. They now laugh and say, "If we ever go to hell again, we will run through faster than the devil knows we are there!" Their sense of humor is amazing for part of the childhood they both had.

The two were the only children to a couple who were extreme alcoholics. They were only a year apart in age, just thirteen months to be exact. Many times they were mistaken for twins. If they had been born in the same year, they could say they were Irish twins, but alas, they were not. They did feel like they were two peas in a pod as they were very similar with their likes and desires.

As young children, they had to take care of each other because they didn't get caretaking or love from their mom. They were at a very young age told to be quiet, don't laugh, and don't wake up Mom. While their parents left them alone every night while they drank in the bar down the street, they lived in front of the TV. In the mornings they tiptoed around so as not to make noise, or they would get their mothers wrath, and she would beat them. After any kind of assault like that, they would huddle together, holding on for dear life to each other and stifle their cries for fear of another beating.

Until their mom had her morning fifth of vodka, they could not make noise. If she was awaken by the sounds of the TV, laughter from them, or dropping an item on the linoleum, they would then pay heavily.

It doesn't take a child long to live like this until they realize they are not loved or were wanted. All they had was each other. They made it through the terror of their mom just to have their dad smack them when he got home because of how their mom told him what bad girls they were. They tried to do what their mom wanted, but they always messed it up. If she wanted a cup of coffee brought to her, they would spill it on the way to her. If she wanted buttered toast, they would burn it. Little did they know as children that you can scrape the burned part off, and then the toast would be fine. Needless to say, they got hit a lot.

When they got old enough to go to school, they got themselves up and dressed. They ate cold cereal every day, and sometimes without milk as there wasn't any. They put together anything they could find for lunch. It was mostly peanut butter and jelly sandwiches. Their mom would buy large containers of the peanut butter and jelly and wouldn't buy anything else for them until they ate every last bite. Just when they were about finished with the hated apricot jelly, their mother would buy another jar of it as she had no recall of what she had bought before and always shopped when she wasn't sober.

It was the concern of a teacher that changed their lives. When asked by the teacher about the bruises and the fact that she and her sister were seldom bathed and always wore the same dirty clothes all week, they were taken into foster care. They were fortunate to be placed together. Things were not bad with the foster parents. The strict rules of the household were not hard to follow. The girls were clean, fed, and properly cared for. Not having any love shown to them at earlier ages, they didn't know how to show any love to anyone except each other.

They attended church with the foster family and heard for the first time that Jesus loves you. They learned to pray and only prayed for one thing. That was that they didn't have to go back to their parents. They did well in school, and things were like this for three years. One day they were told that their mother had died. She drank herself to death. Neither of them cried about the news. Their only concern was whether or not they had to go live with their father. They were told no, and that brought them great relief.

A few months later, the foster parents called the girls in for a family meeting. They were told that the foster parents had been asked if they would consider taking in two more girls to foster parent. The story was that the two girls were taken from a situation similar to what the two of them had gone through. The foster parents said they would like to help these two girls, but would not do it if it wasn't okay with them. They had never been asked their opinion on any household decision before, and they were very surprised. They asked some questions and found out that the girls were the same ages that they were when they were put into foster care. The new girls were of a different race, and they only knew a little English.

Knowing what their lives were like now and what the change had done for them in foster care, the girls said yes. They both wanted to help the two young girls as they had been helped.

The foster family and the girls bowed in prayer, and the father read aloud from Galatians 5:22, "But when the Holy Spirit controls our lives, He will produce this kind of fruit in us; love, joy, peace, patience, kindness, goodness, faithfulness, gentleness, and self-control." They followed with the Lord's Prayer, and most surprising was the hugs they all exchanged.

The two young girls came, and the household was full of activity. The young girls were very dependent on the two older girls. They bonded real well, and each older girl took responsibility for one of the younger. It was delightful to have playmates and little sisters to talk with and teach things to. They all were very close and did most everything together. They loved going to the movies, the state fair, and music venues. They had many wonderful years together as the four sisters.

When they graduated from high school and went to college, they still stayed close. Each of them did separate things, but everyone chose a field to do something for their fellow man or help in some way. The oldest girl went into social services, and after finding a job with the foster care advocacy, she knew she had found her life goal. She would be the eyes and the help for children in foster care and would protect and do everything she could to help children much like herself as a child. The second oldest got her degree in teaching. She specialized with the special needs children and found that she truly loved working with the special children she would work with. Neither of the older girls would marry or have children of their own.

The two younger girls were very artistic and followed their dreams to be a beautician and a master chef. Both going to beauty school and culinary school, they landed jobs in their fields and had special people in their lives.

The four sisters made a promise that each year, they all four would get together and have a "sisters weekend." They would contact one another and pick a date in the late spring or early summer and would plan for a four to five-day reunion. This time was special to them as they would shop, cook, go to movies, fix hair, talk, and reminisce about their lives. They always had a lot to talk about as each of them had different professions.

Today the two sisters have a little joy in their step as the two younger sisters and they will have their annual sisters weekend starting off tomorrow with the culinary chef sister coming in from the coast to join the three sisters who live and work locally. They will laugh and cry and be happy that they have one another as one mixed-up family but one great blessing for having one another.

25

Dragonfly Songs

Today is a lovely day, and the heat from the sun has warmed everything nicely. I have never seen so many dragonflies in my life. They are flying and landing everywhere. It is obvious to me that there are several types of them as some are quite large and others smaller. They look very magical and have a lightness and joy about them as they fly around the park today.

There is a younger woman walking and texting on a phone coming toward me. She stops and says she has never seen dragonflies like this before, and I agree with her and tell her that it's supercool to see them. She said she just sent a photo to a coworker because it's a strange thing to see so many in one place. I tell her to enjoy this day, and she says for me to enjoy it also. She does a few laps on her walk, and I am able to say hello to her each time we pass.

She is a product of change very much like the dragonfly. Starting out with one goal and then changing quickly to fulfill a deeper calling. She was studying music at the university. Her life goal was to get her degree in music and teach music to children while she continued to sing and perform with the church choir and community choir. She had music in her blood since she was a little girl. She would sign up for the community concert society and go to all the special performances. She loved the singers, but the musicians were just as exciting to hear.

She begged her parents to let her take piano lessons when she was in third grade. Her parents, not having the money to buy a piano and not thinking she would stick with it, were able to find a piano teacher who would let her come practice at her house in the mornings before school. It was all she needed to start the music career she dreamed of. So early each school day, she would wake and walk two blocks to the music teacher's house. She would practice for a half hour and then would walk four blocks to school. She would have her music lesson on Saturday mornings at ten o'clock. She would watch cartoons on TV until it was time to walk to the music lesson. She did this her whole third grade year. She never realized at the time that this was the start of a lifetime of music. She just wanted to do it, and to her, it was fun.

She participated in talent shows, school concerts, and of course, church. She was chosen for solos, and she had a lot of fun with these.

At an early age, her father left her mom, and she and her sister and mom were able to get by as her mom had a good job with the government. She was able to keep her spirits up with the music in her life and the friends she had made. Her sister, on the other hand, had gone down a darker path and had gotten in trouble and had a bad reputation for the things she did. Every time her sister got kicked out of school for smoking or skipping class, she felt like she didn't even know who she was. Her sister surrounded herself with kids with problems, and trouble was always around.

Her mom started having memory problems and very often forgot essential things. She didn't mind being called by her aunt's name, but she felt bad when her mom had to ask her who she was. As she got into junior high and her sister got into high school, she had to stand up for herself. There were people who would judge her by her sister's actions. She thought that notion as unfair. She then tried harder than ever to distance herself from her sister and her lifestyle. Her mother didn't stop her sister from dropping out of school and moving in with the group of friends she hung out with. Her mother had no interest in much of anything and took early retirement as her mental lapses were affecting her job. She became somewhat of her mother's caretaker. Her sister had no interest in helping in any way.

It came as no surprise that during her junior year in high school, her sister gave birth out of wedlock to a little girl. Her niece was a precious thing, and the child helped her relationship with her sister for a while. She would get the child, and she and her mom would babysit and entertain the child most weekends. Her sister at times seemed to push the child off on them. Her mother and she had the little girl a lot.

The next few years were a music major's dream as she got music scholarships at high school graduation. She continued to participate in church choir and community choir events. Her freshman and sophomore years in college were very exciting for her. Her mother was failing terribly, and she had to ask for help. Her church body was generous with caretaking for her mom while she attended class. She had fun evenings with her niece, and weekends were full of guiding her mom and household chores.

Her sister turned to an even darker side and was not nice to her mother. She was constantly losing jobs, getting arrested, thrown in jail, and needing money for bail and lawyers. She wasn't taking care of her daughter right. She was draining her mother financially. Something had to end.

With her mother's memory health issues, she worked with the women from the church and her mom's doctors to get the information to have her mom put into assisted living. As much as she hated this, she knew it had to be done. There was a lot on her plate with taking care of her mom's affairs. Her sister was a constant obstacle in helping her. When she had her mom settled into the assisted living facility, she could somewhat breathe easy, but the coming story of chaos in her sister's life was all a life-changer for her.

One night she was called at 2:00 a.m. The local law enforcement agency had her sister in jail along with her housemates. This was serious charges, and she was being called to get her niece. If she was unable to take the child, they would put her in foster care. She raced to the jail and made the connections to get her niece. It was very scary for the child, and she was physically shaking with sobs. She promised her niece that she would take care of her, and she took her home and let her sleep next to her in her bed.

This happened for the next few nights. Missing class at college until she could figure out a plan was very hard on her. Having always been a good student and never missing practice, her life had just been turned upside down. She knew she had to have some help and counseling. She went to visit her pastor and ask some questions that he might be able to help her with. She explained what had happened and wanted to know her legal rights. She was guided to seek permanent guardianship and power of attorney from her sister. She knew she could do this.

Without a source of income, she was faced with quitting college to get a job. She told the pastor that she had no choice but to do what was right for the sake of her niece and that she could possibly return to college at a later time to finish her degree. She cried about her dream being washed away by the avalanche of problems her sister had created in her life. She had promised the child that she would take care of her, and she would find a way. The pastor reminded her that she had a powerful savior on her side, and with him, all things are possible. She left feeling better but not knowing what she would do for a job.

Singing helped her during times of worry, so she and the niece sang a lot. Every song from *The Sound of Music* and other great musicals were taught to the niece. She let her niece sing for her supper, and they sang in the rain. Every other night they would go visit her mother. Most times her mother didn't know who she was, but would enjoy the little girl, thinking it was her own young daughter. It was heartbreaking, but the visits they had were happy and joyful. They would end each visit with a new song or a favorite song she had been teaching her niece.

After choir practice one evening, the husband of one of the choir women walked up to her and said he would like to speak to her. She had seen him many times in church and knew he was a local dentist with a good practice in town. He said he had heard she was looking for a job, and he needed to hire someone to help out his dental assistants. She was surprised he asked her as she knew nothing about this business. He explained that she would be trained on the job and would she consider his offer. She didn't hesitate to say yes, and they agreed for her to come in the next morning for paperwork. She couldn't believe it! This was not what she was expecting to do. So with thanks, she shook his hand and said she would work hard for him. He responded that he knew she would.

She very much liked her job and working with the fine people at the dentist office. She knew right away that the dentist had made the position for her. She hoped the other employees and staff would remain her friends and that she could prove to them that she was a hard worker and that she was a team player.

Once a week, when she was not visiting her mother, she went to the jail to visit her sister during visiting hours. With no money for bail, a lawyer, and with the charges against her, her sister was in jail for a long time. Then once her trial took place, she was not sure if she would be out before her niece was a teenager. She refused to bring the niece to the jail as it went against her core belief of protecting the child. Her sister lived with denial, and there was so much hatred in the way she spoke. She told her sister that maybe she should reconnect with God. That he works in mysterious ways. Just look what he had done in her life.

She was met with foulmouthed hatred and told she was full of pompous bragging and that she hated her. The young woman just shook her head and said to her sister, "When you're rotten about yourself, you become rotten to everyone else, even those you love. Don't worry about me and your daughter. She is in good hands with love all around her. I won't be pawning her toys for drugs, and I'll help her with her prayers each night and pray for you. So I'll let you alone with your negativity, and I will not be a part of this. Goodbye." And she walked out.

That was the last time she went to the jail. Her sister's actions had totally changed her life. She would not have done anything different. She was happy with how things had changed for her. Instead of teaching singing, she was helping people with their teeth and mouths. Two very important keys to singing! She had her mother to visit, her friends at the college and work, and a good job, thanks to a pastor who looked out for her and a fellow parishioner who created a job for her.

She walks in the park today on her lunch break enjoying seeing the dragonflies and wishing they would still be there on the weekend so she can bring her niece to see them. She knows how magical they look, and it gives her an idea to teach her niece a new song about a magical dragon.

26

Third Time Around

TODAY AS I WALK I see some teenager skateboarders coming at me on the path. They are polite enough to jump off of their boards before they get to me. I shake my head and say, "You know, you guys are not supposed to be on this path." They all know this; it is quite obvious. They tell me that they are just trying to get to the road that meanders through the park. The road gives the driving public a chance to slowly view the park as they drive a large loop. I respond with, "Well, good luck. It's right over there, and you are real close." They laugh and take off. I see them later skateboarding on the roadway.

Very often the officers of the law do a drive-through. I hope they enjoy the drive-through for pure pleasure as the only crime that takes place is by the people who do not stay off the walkways with bikes, Rollerblades, and skateboards; and the vandalism of the park benches and tables. Sometimes boards are deliberately broken off. The park service personnel are great about fixing and making repairs right away.

I am approached by an older man wearing a sport hat, shirt, and shorts. They are of the latest rage for fashion attire for men. I say hello, and he responds with, "Nice day!" I say "Yes, it is" and walk on.

He is walking today as he needs to reinvent himself because what he did previously did not work out. As a kid, he grew up with a very successful father who was a high achiever. He and his only sibling brother were expected to be seen and not heard. As important as his dad was as a political figure and business owner, his father spent little time with him and his brother. His mother was a stay-at-home wife, but spent most of her time doing the proper and civic volunteerism for community projects and/or fund-raising for his father's campaigning.

His brother and he had a lot of idle time on their hands as kids and didn't have to worry about adult supervision. He hung out with a few boys who had parents who were not as involved with their offspring, just like his folks. They always found things to do that sometimes got them in trouble.

They got caught throwing rocks and breaking windows out at a downtown warehouse. They had to pay the owner for replacement windows. They got caught breaking bottles in a back alley. They had to come back and clean up all the glass. They got caught stealing baseball cards at the five-and-dime and had to pay back the owner by washing his front windows and sweeping the gutter and front sidewalk—to the owner's satisfaction—for a whole week.

As years went by, the group got in trouble for skipping school and smoking, as well as petty theft. While in high school, they turned their attention to girls and cars. Speeding tickets and traffic violations were a constant. He clashed with his dad, and they argued a lot. His father constantly reminded him that they had a family reputation to uphold. His dad would say how disappointed he was as each bit of trouble he got in furthered the separation in their relationship.

One night his friends and he had the great idea to rob a gas station. They made a plan that they felt was perfect. The young man would borrow his father's pistol so that they had strong persuasion to get the cash. They agreed that there would not be bullets in the gun because they didn't want anyone hurt, they just wanted to use it for muscle. He and one buddy would enter and demand the cash. One buddy would stay in the car to drive, and another buddy was the lookout on the outside of the station. At midnight they felt the time was right as there were no customers at the pumps getting gas or inside the station. They parked to the side of the building, and the deal was on.

He was nervous, and the stocking cap facemask was limiting his eyesight. As they entered and made their demand, the clerk was uncooperative at first. With the gun pointed at the clerk, she opened the cash drawer and promptly released the lock on it, and everything fell to the floor. The young man and his buddy had to get down and scoop the money up off the floor. In doing so, he set the gun down on the cash register and used both hands to fill the bags they had. In their hurry to leave, as fate would have it, he ran out without the gun.

When his father was notified that the registered gun in his name was left at the robbery, the fury in him was tremendous. Being in a position of political clout, he was able to reimburse the business owner and have charges dropped against his son if he put him in a military boarding school. He made the arrangements, and within a day, the young man was shipped out of state, fulfilling the promise to the local law and the business owner.

The boy hated the school and being away from his friends. He stuck it out, and when he graduated, he further defied his father and joined the navy instead of his family's military tradition of being in the air force. He was full of anger, and as the military was a good place for angry young men, you could say it was his saving grace.

He was shipped to Japan. He spent most of all his military career there. He really liked it at first, but as time went on, he really got tired of the food and wished for potatoes and gravy and Mexican burritos. When his hitch was up and he returned home, he found that his parents were proud of him, but there was a distance between him and them. He went to work in the local area for a TV station. He had worked with communications in the service and was able to fit in nicely with the local news team program production.

He married, and after his wife had their third son, she stated she was not willing to fill their backyard with boys looking for a girl. He felt the responsibilities of fatherhood and prayed his boys would not give him the trouble he gave his parents.

After his parents had had a very long political and business ownership career, they were ready to retire. They asked him and his brother if they would be interested in continuing their business. With this opportunity to possibly please his father, he agreed with his brother to take over. He would be the public relations and sales person, and his brother would take care of the bookwork. Learning the ins and outs of the business, he felt very good about his decision to change careers. He got along well with his brother, and the business continued to be profitable, and he and his brother were personally doing well.

Many years passed, and he was never worried that anything would go wrong. His boys were growing up, and he was very active in their lives, unlike how he was raised. One day, the accountant for the business called him and said he would like a private meeting with only him. He was a little surprised, but not worried. They met for lunch, and he was hit with a thunderbolt when the accountant said that he believed his brother was embezzling money from the business. When he questioned why he felt this, the accountant explained that an account was set up with a vendor and there were constant checks written to pay for supplies. All inventories did not reflect these supplies. When the accountant researched the matter further, he discovered that the business didn't exist. He felt that it was a front for his brother to skim from the company. Needless to say, the man was shocked and then furious. He wanted to know how long it had been going on and how much was deposited into the bogus account.

He decided to keep quiet about what he had been told until he had the figures from the accountant. When he was given the information, he was just sick. Over a quarter million dollars was diverted to the fraudulent account. He felt like an idiot for not being more on board with the accounting his brother was doing. He had to confront his brother.

The next morning, he went into the office and shut the door. His brother was happy to see him, but quickly realized by the look on his face that there was a problem. When the man told his brother what he knew, he didn't mince his words with how furious he was with him for the embezzlement. He said that today, one of them would leave the business. The brother was not apologetic at all. He simply said that figures do not lie, but liars can figure. He said he did it because he could. The man told his brother that he could leave with the money he stole and no charges would be brought against him, or he could pay him the quarter of a million dollars that he stole as well as his half of the business and he would leave instead. With that on the table, the brother said that he didn't want to leave the business and that he would buy him out and pay back the quarter of a million dollars.

With that, the man went to a lawyer and had papers drawn up to reflect the sale. He received the stolen money amount after negotiations with the bank. The rest of the buyout was a payment plan reflecting over the next ten years. After one year, his brother filed bankruptcy, and he was not able to collect anything more.

He hadn't known what to do when he first left. He spent a lot of time golfing. Mostly he thought about how naïve he had been and how his brother was so smug about cheating him. He was so angry and disappointed at his brother. How was he going to free himself from this in his mind? Golfing helped, but nothing helped when he tried to sleep and his mind kept bothering him.

He is walking today on the path thinking about his next move. Having to make a big change as he had done twice previously was again a bit scary. At his age, he didn't know if his hiring prospects would be good.

Knowing that he moved into a different direction and that his life was changed both times he reinvented himself before, he was going to look into work that would be satisfying. This time he would be careful not to make a misstep, and he would definitely be law-abiding and on the right path to be a good citizen and father figure to his sons. Seeing an officer of the law cruise by on the street as he walked at the front of the park, he wondered if maybe the local police department needed a communications employee and if they were hiring.

Enhancing the Future

MUSIC IS IN THE AIR. Summer concerts and individuals play to small groups of listeners in a planned event or a perchance private concert. Not everyone has the gift of music given to them, but most have the joy of enjoying music played or sung by others.

Two women are walking and talking. They are catching up, so to speak. After years of living in different states, one of the women just recently moved back to this city. I say hello and am greeted with warm smiles and hellos.

When very young girls, the two women were the best of friends. Having met in second grade, they sat by each other and shared a locker. Each girl had similar interests to each other, but the main bond was music. From very young ages, they dreamed together of being in their own band. To them it would be the best career ever and they would be great. They planned their lives and how their successful music careers would pay for everything they hoped for.

They did all the grade school stuff together over the years. Each got a guitar and each took lessons. They practiced together and both sang. Having different voices, they harmonized well together. One girl's voice was a soft, breathy, floating voice; and the other girl's voice was hauntingly sad, or so her mother said. Each took turns being the lead vocal on songs that were classic or modern favorites.

When they were young preadolescent girls, they were always together at one or the other's house. Each would help the other do her chores. One girl would dampen down the ironing as the other girl would do the ironing. After an hour had gone by, if the job wasn't completed, they would bundle up the predampened clothes into a plastic bag and pop it in the freezer. This was to prevent mildew on the clothes. The next time the ironing needed done, they would retrieve the bag, let the frozen clothing thaw a bit, and iron them. The one girl ironed every Monday and Thursday.

The funny thing that happened once was the girl who ironed was asked by her dad where his favorite golf shirt was. She remembered she had put it in the bag in the freezer the previous day. She told him it was in the freezer! Her mom and she laughed so hard when the look on his face was a look at her like she had gone nuts. Her mother explained the principle behind it to him, and he had a good chuckle too. From that point on, her family referred to their clothes as warm or freezer material.

The other girl had vacuuming and dusting as chores. Each girl would do her part to finish quickly so they could go play music.

When they hit junior high, they were constantly dreaming of their big music careers. Nothing would stop them, they said—until something did.

During eighth grade, one of the girls' parents divorced. It wasn't a difficult divorce, and the girl was to live with her mom and go live with her dad for two months in the summer. What was a difficulty was her dad moved many states away, and her having to be gone from her friend for two whole months would just kill her. Not only would she hate leaving her friend, but their music practice sessions would have to be put on hold until she got back. Thinking about this was misery. Knowing she could do nothing about it was even worse.

As summer approached and school got out for the summer, her once excitement for summer vacation had a big black cloud over it. After just a couple of weeks at home, she was put on a plane to fly to her father's. That year her dad tried to do just about everything he could to make her happy. She would have none of it. Her madness at her parents for putting her into this predicament was not going to wear off easily. She wrote a lot of letters to her friend and got a few to read sent to her. She marked the days off the calendar until she could return home. The days dragged by, and she swore she would never come again.

The day came to leave, and she smiled for the first time since coming. She made her father feel bad, and she knew it. At this point, she didn't care about his feelings or life.

When she got home, her friend was there to greet her, and her happiness returned one hundred percent. There was now a song in her voice and a dance in her step. With a few weeks until school started, she and her friend practiced their music and picked up where they had left off with big dreams for their successful music careers.

The school year was really fun for the girls as being in high school presented different opportunities. They got to play at a talent show their class put, on and their music was well received. They felt that they were on their way to music stardom, and those thoughts filled their heads.

As the freshman year came to a close, she had to face the reality that she had to leave for two months in the summer again. She was hating it, but there was nothing she could do about it. This time when she flew down to see her dad, she was met at the airport by her dad and his new girlfriend. Not wanting to like anything about being with her dad, she instantly decided that she didn't like the girlfriend. She wouldn't even try.

She knew her dad was uncomfortable with her ignoring any attempt by him or the girlfriend to polite conversation. She didn't care. Her dad and mom created this hell for her, and they were going to know it. She wasn't about to play nice. Again, the summer dragged by, and her dad tried to get her to ease up. She wanted him to suffer, just like she was suffering. Her happiest day would be the day she was leaving.

Back home, she again rejoiced to be reunited with her friend. Their friendship bond was tighter than ever. They decided to get matching tattoos. She knew her mother wouldn't care, but her friend knew that her parents would disapprove of it, so they would put it in a place where she could hide it. They chose a yellow rose tattoo to be put just behind their shoulder. Her friend could hide it by not wearing sleeveless shirts and not turning her back to her mom when she was showering. It was a great plan. Their secret was a delight to them, and they wrote a song about a secret love.

That Christmas break, she was told that she was flying down to her dad's as he wanted her at his wedding. She didn't want to go, but knew that this time was only for a few days. It wouldn't be so bad, she thought. The bad part was now she was going to have a stepmom, and she didn't like her. She wished her parents would quit screwing up her life. She told herself that she wouldn't try to like her. She just wouldn't.

At the airport, her dad looked as happy as she had ever seen him. He gushed over her how big she was getting and how pretty she was. She withheld her thanks. The wedding ceremony was on a beach, and a few guests and family attended. Everyone congratulated her for getting a new stepmom and voiced their opinion that the stepmom was a really nice person. The young woman didn't care, she wasn't going to like her.

When she returned home, she couldn't wait to tell her friend how cool it was to have a beach wedding. She pretty much decided that when she married, she would have a beach wedding too! She admitted that that was one thing her stepmom had done right.

School flew by, and again it was time to pick the dates to go to her dad's for two months. How she hated picking this time out of her summer. She absolutely didn't want to go, but could do nothing about it. When her dad met her at the airport, he was without his wife. He said he wanted to talk to her alone. He told her that he knew why she is mad. He said that he hoped that this being the third year, she could try to enjoy herself. He said he knew she didn't like her stepmom, but that she hadn't even given her a chance. He said, "She is not your mom, but I hope she could be your friend." There was no intent from him or his new wife to have her replace her mother. The girl listened, but did not speak as what he said was true. She hadn't even tried to give her stepmom a chance. Then her dad said, "My wife can be your friend if you let her. I want you to show her respect always. I will not be put in the middle between you two. You, as a daughter I dearly love, must either accept my life choice or you are out of it. It's your choice. I suggest you choose wisely."

At that he drove to his house where her stepmom had made a lovely meal. She had a lot to think about, and she felt ashamed that she had not been real nice to her stepmom in the past. She made her mind up, that for her father's sake, she would try. Two weeks later, her father got the call he never dreamed would happen. His ex-wife was on the phone telling him that she would no longer be the custodial parent. He would have to keep the girl as she was leaving and would not be there when the girl returned from the summer visitation. When the father asked why this had come about, the mother said that he had a better life now that he was remarried. She was no longer interested in being a parent, and this was a chance for a clean break.

Needless to say, he was going to have his hands full telling his daughter she would be staying permanently because her mother had abandoned her. It was a nightmare. For every hateful thought she had for her dad, her hatred for her mom was tenfold. She had ruined her life. She destroyed her plans and dreams. She abandoned her like throwing away a piece of trash. How could she do that to her own daughter? How was she going to survive? She was devastated. Her rage was monumental. She knew she would never forgive her mom. She cried a river and screamed at God. She was beyond crushed.

Her father made all the arrangements to transition her into his life as now it would be her life too. He sought legal and spiritual help. His heart broke for his daughter. He would do everything possible to make this work.

Summer was a mind-numbing blur for his daughter. She was registered for school in the fall with her dreams destroyed and her best friend gone from her life. She didn't feel much of anything. School started her junior year. It was very different than her previous school. She had made up her mind that she wasn't going to like anything here in this school, but she found out that she did like some things. There was the music. Different music. Music with a Latin influence and an island, calypso vibe. It was free and easy. Being a guitar player, she was able to fit in and find friendship with fellow musicians. The music here was upbeat. This helped her lift her spirits as her anger was still immense.

She made it perfectly clear to her dad that she would never forgive her mom. He was okay with that for the first year, but by her senior year, he began working on her to try and forgive. She didn't understand how she could forgive someone who hadn't asked for forgiveness. How could she forgive her mom for destroying her future plans and dreams? For abandoning her? Her dad said that her anger was eating her up and that forgiveness would stop the anger. Then he said the words that were music to her ears. Words that she would live by. Words that she would embrace. "Forgiveness does not change the past, but it does enhance the future."

She threw her arms around her dad and thanked him for being there for her. She had chosen wisely before, and she wisely would choose to forgive.

Her senior year was busy, and her heartbreak of losing her best friend and her dreams were replaced with playing music in outdoor parks with her friends and joining a group of musicians who play at community events. It was like being in a band, but not making big money. It was just fun.

After a fun summer, she and a fellow musician struck up a friendship. They would play music together and write songs. She very often recalled her best friend when the two of them played together. She found common ground with her stepmom. Happiness slowly came back into her life. She was a pen pal with her former best friend. They started out writing all the time, but it changed to maybe once a month. Her music and love interest partner worked in house construction, building high-end houses as his main job. His music hobby kept them both happy and busy on the weekends.

She did have the beach wedding, and her new husband played a beautiful song he had written for her after the vows were said. It was his love song to her, and it contained a line about forgiveness. They thanked God for finding each other.

They had some really great years before they had children bless their lives. Watching the news one day, she saw that there was a tremendous need for carpenters in the area she had grown up. With the economic area booming and a rebuilding of some communities due to a natural disaster, she asked her husband if he would be interested in moving there. She and he researched the civic and cultural information on her former city and were pleased that it could be a new adventure. They made the decision to relocate. She was extremely happy to reunite with her childhood friend.

Today in the park as like many days, they walk and catch up with stories. She is listening to her friend tell her how her parents found out about her tattoo. She is laughing about how clever they thought they were, when in reality, it was silly to think she could possibly hide her tattoo. They make plans to come to the park the next evening as her husband will play with a local group of musicians for the park audience. The love of music kept them friends for many years. Now the music of friendship is their joy to be shared with each special time they get together.

Paddling Along

As I walk today, the clouds are gathering, and the air feels like it just might rain. I spy a mother duck and her little ducklings drifting along in the river water. They seem to just go with the flow, no hurry to go anyplace, just naturally drifting along. As a few raindrops start to fall, I think how the ducks won't be affected by the rain at all, they will just let the rain roll off their backs, and they will continue to slowly paddle along with no worries.

I am approaching a man who is jogging. His face has lines of stress and worry, and he only nods at me when I say hello.

His jog in the park is to calm his aching heart. And to think. Lately, life dealt a heavy hand to him and his wife. After so many years of trying and many specialists and money spent, they had just had their third miscarriage. The devastation of this lost child and their attempts to have a family has crushed both their spirits. His wife's constant crying and the ache he feels pushed him out of the house to come clear his brain with a jog.

It just seems so unfair, and he is trying not to be mad at God, but he feels let down, disappointed, and unsure how to act or react with his wife. This whole thing has been a roller coaster of emotions for both of them.

The first pregnancy was the result of many years of waiting so they could get their ducks in a row, so to speak. They wanted job security, money in the bank, a nice home, and nice vehicles. Both doing their fair share to accomplish this, they had the plan in place after six years of marriage. When they decided to try and start, they had difficulties and finally sought a specialist after two years of failed attempts on their own. With a few lifestyle changes and close monitoring of their health, they were able to conceive.

The day they took the pregnancy test was as scary as it was exciting. With the positive result, they told the world their good news. All family and friends heard it first from them. They were so happy, and plans were put in place to get everything they would need for their first child. They poured over catalogues and websites to design the perfect baby nursery. Not wanting the doctors to tell them the sex of the child, they were even more excited to have the big surprise at the birth.

When his wife started noticing problems and having difficulties, they sought medical help. They were not prepared for the possibility that this baby would not come to them, so reality hit them hard. The doctor explained that sometimes this happens and that they would be able to try and succeed again.

It was hard on them emotionally to now have to tell all family and friends that they had lost the child. It was really hard for his wife, as she blamed herself. She struggled with issues of failure, and it took quite a while before she could smile again or to laugh. They took things easy and decided that if and when they conceived again, that it would be more private this time. They felt that exposing their personal life, hopes, dreams, and desires was putting too much emotion out, and they didn't want to have to go through the retraction pain again.

So his wife dusted and straightened the nursery each day, and they held on to each other for support. They stayed busy with their employment and a few civic activities. He played with a group of guys on a baseball team, and she was involved with a nonprofit organizing 4K walks and races to help the less fortunate.

They were nervous and took their time. Many months later, she knew she was again pregnant. They were a bundle of nerves when they bought another pregnancy test. With a lot of talking to God to make their dream come true, they watched for the results. When the positive result showed, they wept in each other's arms. Keeping their word to be more private, they said nothing to anyone. They finished up purchasing items for the nursery and took special care to make sure they would be prepared parents. One night while sleeping, his wife woke him and told him he needed to help her as she was again experiencing a difficulty. He helped her dress and got her to the car. He drove too fast, out of fear, but made it to the all-night emergency room. After a long-drawn-out night with no sleep and no hope for a good outcome, they lost the child.

Again, they plunged into hopelessness and dark despair. Tears came like a river to his wife. He tried to cry on the inside to be strong for her on the outside.

They had a long hard time of emotional recovery as they had no outside support because no one knew. The decision to be private backfired with the heaviest of burdens upon them only. She was very fragile now, and even seeing a baby on TV would start her crying. They struggled through most days and held each other at night.

They made an attempt to be positive after months of sadness. He could not walk by the nursery without a pain in his heart, so he closed the door. It was better for him to have it out of sight, so out of mind.

They planned vacations and holiday trips and meals. They did everything to fit in and be normal and to pretend that everything was perfect in their lives, but the truth was that he would break inside when he would look into his wife's hungry eyes. It just killed him to see her without the one thing she wanted.

They slowly recovered some happiness. Getting a dog was very helpful for companionship. His wife and the dog were running partners, and she now had another to care for besides himself. She told him that sometimes when she ran, she didn't know if she was running to a new life or away from pain. She hadn't figured it out yet, but the dog gave her a reason to smile. She now had to keep plugging along, one foot in front of the other, each day.

Over a year later, his wife again knew she was pregnant. The feelings of apprehension, fear, and anxiety overwhelmed the emotions of happiness and joy. Just to be on the safe side, they made an appointment with her doctor. After a thorough physical exam, it was determined that she was indeed again pregnant. The doctor wanted to take good precautions as she had not carried past her first trimester in the past. He ordered up bed rest and wanted them to come in every two weeks for checkups. This was not going to be easy to do without telling her mom and his. So they decided that only their parents would know, and siblings and friends would not.

Things went well for the first few weeks with the doctor appointments. There was nothing to raise a red flag about. Toward the start of the second trimester, his wife had cabin fever something fierce. She was antsy to go stretch her legs and walk the dog. She begged him to let her go and just take a walk. He, with much hesitation, agreed that if she walked, not jogged, she could go with the dog and enjoy getting out. He knew it would do a body good to get out of the house. Little did he know that as she would step off the curb to cross a street, she would twist her ankle and fall. Not knowing it would happen, she fell to her side and not forward to her hands and knees. She landed heavily on her hip. Being in good physical shape, she bounced up and was only concerned about her ankle and not spraining it further. She turned around and started for home. She could feel the pain deep inside and prayed she just shook things up and didn't tear or break anything.

Going ever so slowly, she made it home. Once she sat down to rest, she could hardly control her heartbeat and breathing. She was again living in fear. She knew she had to call her husband and felt that he would be mad at her. She called her mom first. It helped her to have her mom tell her to breathe and to practice relaxing yoga mind-calming thoughts. It helped a lot, and she was able to call her husband.

She phoned him at work, and with sobbing in her voice, she related her fall. He asked her if she was all right, and she responded, "Somewhat." Fear was her biggest problem. He told her he would be right home. Soon after, he arrived and helped her cold-press her ankle and make her comfortable on the couch. He helped her change her clothes and fed and watered the dog before he started dinner preparations. His wife cried lightly the whole time. It didn't matter what he said, she would blame herself if something happened to the baby.

Again in the night she woke him to help her as she again was losing the baby. He got her dressed and carried her to the car and then drove to the emergency room. Early in the morning, he called both sets of parents with the unfortunate news. Her mother said she would come over and stay with her. His parents were also filled with sadness and reassured him that somewhere out in this big world, there is a baby for them. Just give it time.

He knew what they meant and was grateful for his and his wife's health and life they had. He knew they would try again and maybe look into alternatives for being parents.

His wife struggled more than ever with blame. He just didn't know what he could say to her to make her feel better.

As he jogged on the path today, his mom called and asked him how he was doing and if things were better with his wife, as it had been awhile since the accident. He said he was torn up still on the inside but would paddle along against the landslide of tears his wife was living. He said he just didn't know what to do for her, so he was jogging in the park to burn anxiety. His mom reminded him that it wasn't what he could say at this time, it was what he would do that mattered most. He said goodbye and thought about what his mom said and let the rain fall down on him as the clouds broke and the rain would wash away his tears. As with the ducks, he would let the rain roll off his head and face; On the outside, he would be calm and collected, but as the ducks' feet keep paddling under the water, he will let his inner turmoil keep him paddling along. The words of a song came to him about leaving a cake out in the rain and they would never have that recipe again, and he knew that he was going home to take his wife in his arms as he had married not only the woman he could live with, but the one he couldn't live without.

29

Right Place

SEVERAL TIMES A YEAR THERE are fund-raiser runs in the park. Different groups have fun runs of a 5K or half marathon. Prior to the run, there is new spray paint on the walking trail to mark the runner's progress. Such as 1/4 or 1/2 way done. Setting up a refreshment table at the beginning and end of the run are volunteers.

As I walk by them, I say hello to a lady who says hello back, and I continue on.

She is not running the race today. She has run all her life. Not races exactly, but running around after four children and doing all the volunteer work she could possibly do.

It all started when she was young and she would volunteer for anything the teacher or the neighbors or the coaches would ask for a volunteer. Running errands was in her blood. As often as she volunteered, she was chosen. She got a good reputation of being one they could count on, no matter what the task was.

While in school, she was on every committee. Whether it was decorating for the dance, being on the sign-up for everything committee, the planning committee, or the cleanup committee. She was always there. Everyone could count on her. In high school, she was a class officer and was a member of the school newspaper, yearbook team, and graduation planning team. All of this while holding down a part-time job at the local greasy spoon and leading her church Bible study for the youth.

Not a day went by that she wasn't doing something for someone. She would babysit if someone was in a bind and dog walk if the elderly neighbor's regular dog walker had to have the day off. Once she graduated, she jumped into the college scene with full gusto. Every issue that the student body needed volunteers, her hand was up in the air and her feet hit the ground running. Every cause that was near and dear to her heart was her calling to jump in and help. Delivering flyers, printing inserts, answering phones, being a greeter, making cookies, keeping records for right to life, politicians, cancer, March of Dimes, and animal rescue. Every cause or fund-raiser would have her front and center or behind the scenes helping and running around.

After college, she married a fellow she met as volunteers for a nonprofit for the less fortunate. He was also interested in helping others, and she was attracted by that. They immediately started a family and, after ten years, had a family of four children. Her life then became running with the children and every church, sport, school, and summertime activity or program she could be involved with. She was the class mom, the lunch lady volunteer, the playground monitor, the VBS teacher, the team mom, and of course, a Sunday school teacher. One day her husband asked who she was baking for. She said it was the last day of swim lessons, and the kids would all eat in the park afterward, and she was bringing the cookies and ice cream. He then asked what she would be involved in next. She didn't give it any thought as she had already signed up to help the oldest boy's baseball team with practice sessions and the youngest daughter's Girl Scout troop was needing her to coordinate a community food drive. Her husband asked her to set aside some time for a vacation later in the summer as he wanted to go on a trip with the kids before school started. She said okay and checked her calendar to see what she was going to have to juggle to make his request work.

In an attempt to keep her home cleaned and all the household chores done, she invented a challenge for herself and the kids. She called it the Chinese Fire Drill. She would gather the children in the kitchen and give each child a chore. One would get to vacuum the living room, one would clean the downstairs bathroom, one would clean the upstairs bathroom, and the last would sweep the kitchen floor and empty all the wastepaper baskets and take the kitchen trash out. She would then set the timer for ten minutes, and everyone would grab what they needed to complete the chore and take off to see if they could get their task done in the allotted ten minutes. She would load and unload the dishwasher, wash large cookware, get some meal preparations done, and throw laundry into the washer and switch done clothes to the dryer—all in the allotted time.

Every day the chores were different. Some days they folded clothes and stripped and remade beds. They washed windows inside and out with one child on each side. One would wipe up and down and one side to side. That way if the sun reflected streaks, they would know which side had the streaks.

This hurry-up housecleaning was like a game, but the children learned to work like a team. When the timer went off, they were done. Whatever didn't get done was on her list for the next day. If a job was done poorly, she would work with her child the next day to complete the task properly. This Fire Drill worked well with other areas of their lives too. Getting the kids to change their clothes to go to a function or helping get everything ready for an evening meal, each child had a task to get done.

When they were hurrying around at a fevered pace, she would say, "Time's a wasting, fun awaits."

When they were done, they would load up in the car and head to whatever activity was scheduled for that particular day. In the evenings when they didn't have a function to go to, she would iron while the children read. The younger children would read out loud so she could help them with mispronounced words and with phrasing. Her husband would go over school papers in the winter with the children or play with the kids outside in the summer, playing catch or Frisbee.

Things were always busy like a beehive for her family. This is what she enjoyed, and she slept well every night.

Once she and her husband finalized their summer vacation plans with where they were going and what they would be doing, she was really looking forward to it. A few days later, she was helping the baseball coach with the older boys and was filling in for the batting coach. While distracted by a commotion in the dugout, she was hit in the ribcage by a flying bat that was let go of from a missed ball swing. It hit her extremely hard and knocked her to the ground. Others ran to help her, and she said she was okay, that she just got the wind knocked out of her. As painful as the ribcage was, she found it excruciating to laugh, sneeze, or cough. It was not something she had noticed before, but she would cough a little, and the injury made her aware that she did cough occasionally. She figured she would be okay with only bruised ribs to deal with.

At home that evening, it was painful to inhale deeply. Her husband suggested she get a doctor's appointment and check it out as she probably had a broken rib. She made an appointment with her primary health-care doctor and explained that she was in the wrong place at the wrong time and got hit with the bat. She examined her, listened to her lungs, and ordered an x-ray. The doctor was sure the rib was cracked or broken as she had dark bruising.

While waiting in the waiting room after the x-ray and before the doctor could talk to her about the results, she felt guilty for having to be at the doctor instead of with the baseball team helping with practice. When the doctor met her again, she stated that she had bad news. She looked at her in wonder as a broken rib wasn't all that bad, she thought. The doctor said the x-ray showed a broken rib and a cracked rib, but much more. The doctor showed her the spot in her lung that showed up, and in her opinion, this needed to be attended to right away. She had a lot of questions, and it was decided to do a biopsy in two days.

As her husband and she waited for the results from the biopsy, they prayed for the best outcome and for God's healing. They were not overly surprised when the doctor called them in and she was told that the findings showed she had a rare fast-growing lung cancer. It was caught in time, and with the removal of two-thirds of her left lung, she would be cancer free and able to lead a normal quality life. Her doctor said, "As unlucky as you feel about being in the wrong place at the wrong time, you actually were in the right place at the right time. If you had waited to come see me when your cough was getting real bad, it would have been too late. The cancer would have taken your life."

She sobbed in her husband's arms for thanks and because she was scared to death. This so-called accident was really a blessing in disguise.

They did the surgery, and she was told that they got everything and she would be perfectly fine after her recovery. She felt like dying every time she coughed or sneezed. Her chest hurt so badly when she got hit with the bat, but them sawing her chest cage open was so very painful. While bed recovery was necessary, she hated not getting up and doing anything. All the plans and activities she was missing made her feel terrible. However, many rallied around the family and helped chauffer the children to practices and games. Friends and relatives made meals and cleaned the house. Her husband was busier than ever, but was able to be at her beck and call for anything she needed. Her husband and she had long talks about her taking it easy and that she was going to have to scale back all her volunteerism. They said that the focus would be on being healthy and doing things as a family.

She felt terrible that the planned vacation wasn't going to happen. She would not be healed enough to go on a trip. Her husband reassured her that the following year, they would have a fantastic vacation as she would be fully recovered and up to it. He said that this year, they would be together as a family and vacation right at home. There would be campouts in the backyard with sky watching of the night star constellations, learning where the Big Dipper and the North Star were, and watching satellites cross the starry sky. There would be movie marathons to watch and barbecue picnics to do for everyone who helped them during her surgery and recovery with the kids and the house. He said it was a thanksgiving vacation at home and it would be wonderful. He would take care of everything. She felt happy that he was so wonderful.

She was going to have to learn to say no. Saying no was something she had never done, but now she needed her time. God gave her more time, so she was going to stop and smell the roses at a slower pace than she had ever done before.

Today in the park, she is participating as a volunteer as her husband and children walk the 5K. She will continue on her slower walk through life and enjoy the extra time she was given because of a blessing that put her in the right place at the right time.

30

Forever Entwined

ONCE THE INNER GROWTH PLANTS get real big in between the tall trees, there is a cooler, shady environment in the park. As sunlight filters through the foliage, occasionally you can see a spiderweb. The webs are a work of art with the spider weaving and constructing this intricate choice of home and trap for their food supply. As I walk today, I see a very large web that glistens with the sunrays. There is a sense of mystery and amazement with what the spider has created.

Coming toward me speed-walking is a woman. She has music buds in her ears and waves to me as I say hello as we pass. She has a lot on her mind as a phone call this morning shocked her greatly. Answering the phone, she was told by her best friend's mom that her friend, whom she had grown up with, was found dead that morning in her home. The shock that hit her that someone her very own age was gone, was unreal, but having been the best of friends all their lives, was devastating.

She met her friend when she was in third grade when her folks moved in across the street from her. They met while the moving van was still unloading all her family's furniture. There were several kids all sitting on the sidewalk curb watching the moving guys. Her family were all inside helping put boxes in the proper rooms and unloading boxes into closets and cupboards. She had five brothers and sisters, and there was a lot of activity going on. Once the moving van pulled out, she and her brothers and sisters all went outside to check out the yard and neighborhood. The kids on the curb said hi, and they all met and exchanged names and ages. The kids on the curb were a family of five girls and one boy. She was from a family of four girls and two boys. Most all of the two families had kids the same age. She was the same age as the girl she met. They became friends and then best friends.

All summer long they would ride bikes, make forts in the field in back of her friend's house, play kick the can at night and hide-and-seek. Growing up across the street was real fun as they always found fun stuff to do. They would play beauticians as her friend's mom was a beautician and had a little beauty shop area set up. The mom would let the girls wash and curl and blow-dry their hair. They would listen to the radio and sing to the new pop groups like the Monkees, the Beatles, the Beach Boys, and the Doors. They would run with kites and try to catch the wind. They would chase after rainbows and try to find pots of gold. They would play hospital, office, and of course, beauty pageant.

When they got to be teenagers, they listened to records, poured over dream guy magazines, and did each other's nails. They got in trouble together too. Once they got caught smoking on a backyard sleepover. They had gotten the cigarettes from the friend's dad and got busted when the parents looked out the window into the dark and saw the lighted tips of the cigarettes. They both got grounded, and that two weeks was terrible on them not seeing each other. They would babysit for money, and it allowed them to go to the movies and buy records.

One summer, there was a work program done with the state, and both girls applied. Lower-income families would qualify if they had a lot of kids; and since their families were large, they both got hired. They were going to work at the school doing the summer cleaning. The school janitor put the girls to work scrubbing black marks off the mopboards and cleaning desks. They washed windows and helped scrub floors. They worked cleaning out lockers and cleaning and sanitizing locker rooms.

Each day they would sit down and eat lunch with the older janitors and listen to all the woes of their married or unmarried lives. They had some real characters they worked with. They enjoyed working together and having their friendship. Each day, they walked to work and back home together.

When they were freshmen, they skipped school and went with a boy and drove around in his cool car. They didn't think about how they were going to explain being gone for the afternoon classes. They concocted a plan to lie to the principal about one of them being sick as a dog in the bathroom and the other there to help her. They blamed the sickness on school lunch and possible food poisoning. The principal was a wise man who knew both girls well as good students with no behavior problems. He said he didn't believe them, but he would give them the benefit of the doubt as after all, yesterday's lunch was not that great. Both girls gave a sigh of relief when they knew their parents wouldn't be called. However, the principal warned them that he would not ever again allow them to miss class without a signed note from their folks. If it happened again, he would expel them for three days. Not wanting that to happen, the two of them never violated any school rule again.

When the first homecoming dance came around that they were both going to, they were super excited. They had the beautician mom do their hair, and they had the other mom make the dinner for the girls and their dates to have before the dance. They got dressed together in the dresses they had shopped for together, and they helped each other with their makeup and nails.

They were sisters in spirit and enjoyed doing everything together during their high school years. They comforted each other when a boy would break one of their hearts, and they would rejoice with each other when some guy would ask one of them out, if he was a dreamboat.

When the friend got engaged during Christmas their senior year, it was the most exciting six months for them to plan the wedding. They poured over books for dresses and decorations.

After graduation, which couldn't have come fast enough for either of them, the countdown was on for the wedding. They were on cloud nine with excitement. As the maid of honor for her friend, she had put off making her own after graduation plans. Once the wedding was over, she needed to find a job and get about getting on with her life.

Because she was a good student and an honor student, she was asked to apply at the local job service for a receptionist job. She interviewed and got the job. She was fortunate to have on-the-job training and enjoyed her work very much. She got to meet people from all walks of life looking for employment. This is how she met her future husband. He came in looking for a job with his business degree as his area of interest. She steered him to fill out applications at two local banks who were looking for employees. He was hired and came back to thank her for helping him and asked her out for coffee. Their coffee dates turned into dinner dates and then weekend dates and then setting a wedding date.

The excitement started again with her and her best friend. The planning for the wedding was a double treat for both of them, only reverse this time. The two couples had outings together and became a foursome. The wedding turned out to be everything she ever wanted, and her maid of honor was as happy as she was on her own wedding day.

Years of work, having children, dealing with siblings and parents, and job changes kept the two women busy all the time but constantly in touch.

One day her friend said that she needed to talk to her and would she come over. When they met, she could see that she was a bit upset. Her friend told her that her husband had been offered a position advancement with his employer, but that it meant moving to another town. She was extremely sad to have to move and leave her best friend. Trying to comfort her and calm the sadness she felt by what she just heard, she said that this was not the worst thing. It was a great thing for them. She was happy for them, but super sad to lose her babysitter. They laughed as they both helped each other out that way. They agreed they would always stay in touch and that they would make every effort to visit each other as often as possible.

Life happens, and they didn't stay in touch as much as they thought. They still talked on the phone for their birthdays, anniversaries, and when something happened in either of their families. They sent school pictures of their kids, Christmas cards, and announcements for births, baptisms, confirmations, graduations, weddings, and funerals.

The call this morning made her realize that her younger carefree days were gone, that the detailed web she had spun of her life was totally engrained with her friend and what they had shared as spirit sisters in her youth. She now felt old. All those memories. What a fun friend now gone.

She had agreed to speak at the service for her friend, and she had a million memories to wade through to say the perfect things.

She thinks how as children her friend and she would try to catch the wind, and now her friend was part of it. Forever entwined with each other in the web of friendship they had created, she would love her always.

31

Mother Skills

THE PARK HAS FLOWERS BLOOMING today. Most flowers are really weeds, but any blooming flower is only a weed if it's somewhere you don't want it to be. Among the flowers is the occasional butterfly fluttering around like playful souls. Butterflies are full of endurance and have gone through much change. I like watching the delicate creatures, which make me smile. I am approached by an Asian woman who is just enjoying the sights and sounds and in no hurry whatsoever. She smiles and says hello back as I say my hello.

She has been lost in thought a lot lately. She has herself to talk to, as she has a lot to think about. She came here to enjoy the American experience and found out that she loved it very much and wanted to spend the rest of her life in America. She was able to find work with others of her race and spoke her native tongue. She established some friendships with coworkers. Some coworkers were here on visas and left after a period of time. She applied for citizenship and is working through the process of getting her citizenship. When she told her parents she was going to stay in America, they threw a fit. They were not happy with her at all. Every phone call was an argument. Every phone call to them made her feel guilty, mad, sad, and unhappy. The rest of the time she was happy. She loved this city and America. She just wished her parents could see this place, and maybe they would understand.

In an attempt to be more American, she decided not to do some of the things her culture had taught her. She ate a lot differently, and in this land of plenty, there are a lot of places to eat. Her mother had taught her how to prepare many special dishes, and she had actually gotten very good at preparing a meal. But she didn't do that much anymore as she decided to adopt more American ways.

She missed her parents and really wanted to see them, but had no intention of going back to her native country. She found more and more reasons she wanted to stay just where she was and not turn back to the old country and ways.

Two months ago, her father called and told her that her mother was ill. He had not wanted to tell her previously as he did not want her to feel guilty for being in America. Her mother was more than just ill, she died a few days later, and that's when the guilt started. Unable to leave and knowing there was nothing for her to do, she decided to stay and not return for her mother's service. Her reasoning is that she wanted her memories of her mom, not the final closure of her life to be what runs through her thoughts. She was grateful in a way that she hadn't seen the deterioration of her tiny, petite mom, and she would never have those sad images in her brain. She felt bad for her father and prayed that he would change his mind and come visit her in America.

As she strolled and thought about her childhood, her life in the old country, and her family history, she choked up and cried and cried and cried. It was during one of those sad times that she had a moment of clarity. She decided to think and list all the things her mother had taught her. Even though her mother was not affectionate with her growing up, she did teach her many skills. Her coworkers would compliment her on how cool it was that she could fold napkins like birds or take paper and make beautiful butterflies and fans. She came to it easily, and it always pleased people. She was a good cook too. All learned by watching and working with her mom. "Just practice" was her mom's motto. She practiced a lot, and doing some things were just natural to her now. In remembering the lessons taught by her mom, she realized that her rejection of her culture in this country was going to end. In remembrance of her heritage and her mother's teachings, she would now make the traditional foods. She would do so with thankfulness in her heart and love for her mom, whom she pictured in her mind as young, healthy, and showing her skills she must practice. So she would practice and invite her friends over for an old country meal and thank her mom for teaching her to be like her.

I make my lap around the trail and find her sitting on one of the benches talking in her native tongue to her dad on the phone. As tears rolled down her face, she explained how very nice it would be for him to come see her in America. As I walk, I spy a butterfly and smile at how pretty and delicate they are, very much like a paper one made with practiced hands by a mother who taught her daughter many skills.

32

Fire Success

THERE IS A SLIGHT BREEZE in the park, a sign of things cooling down from the heat of the last few months. There are fewer people in the park as school has started, and the children are not here today. I hear a fire siren off in the distance and know that the good men of the fire rescue units will be on site shortly to help whoever is in need of them. I smile about the thought of a fireman as my brother is one. He loves his job and wanted to be a fireman since he was a little boy.

I greet an older couple with hello, and they smile and return the greeting. They are holding hands while walking and are enjoying the sights and sounds of being in the park today.

They also hear the fire sirens, and it floods them with emotions from long ago when they had a fire that effected their livelihood and personal life. Without the help of the fire rescue, they would have lost their life's work with their diner, and they have great admiration for all firemen and women.

They begin talking about the fire, and they share many memories of their long-ago fire.

When he was a young boy, he and his parents lived behind the diner that his parents owned and worked. It was a local eating diner open seven days a week. His parents were always there, and he was a dishwasher and busboy from an early age. The diner had a local reputation, and either on a daily or weekly basis, they would have repeat customers. He being an only child had grown up in an adult world.

He could carry on a conversation with most any adult, and many patrons sought him out to talk with him.

His folks worked hard with the business with his dad doing most the cooking, his mom the baking, managing the staff, and business matters. The arrangement worked very well, and he daily had chores to do. They closed the business only on Easter and Christmas, and they would close the diner part on the Fourth of July, but have a parking lot BBQ in the afternoon for all their customers, free of charge. They were able to feed all their friends and then clean up and go to the community fireworks show. They did this every year of his child and teenage years.

When he got old enough to do more than wash dishes, his dad worked with him with preparing vegetables, fruits, and meats to make the meals. He was able to continually stock the salad bar and help his dad do some grilling. He found he had a fondness for making the dinner meals, as the breakfast eggs, pancakes, and waffles were not as enjoyable to make. He learned exactly how to cook a steak or burger to the customer's request, and he really enjoyed working with his dad.

While in high school, he asked his dad if they could get a smoker, as he thought smoked meat would be a nice addition to the diner's menu. His father wasn't against the idea; he just didn't feel he could add one more responsibility to his plate.

He reassured his dad that he would learn how to do it correctly and that it would be his area of expertise. So his dad and mom researched the best commercial smoker they could buy, and he researched the best smoking tips, hints, and procedures.

After a little trial and error, they had a successful product, and the customers ordered up a lot of his smoked brisket, pork ribs, and prime rib. They limited the menu to these three items, and the demand kept him busy as all three were very popular.

The summer after high school graduation, he met a real nice waitress who worked the diner on the weekends, as she was still in school. They would talk together on her breaks and go to the local malt shop after her shift was over, if the diner wasn't too busy and his dad would let him go. They dated, and after her graduation two years later, they tied the knot at the justice of peace office on a sunny day in June. His parents closed the diner for the wedding ceremony, and they all went to a very nice meal at a five-star hotel complex. It truly was a first for them all, as they never went out to eat. His father insisted they do this as a wedding present. He was serious that no one would work on this day his son would marry. They did have a lovely meal, but there were a few items served they all knew that his father could make better. The cake his mother made and brought for them to cut was heavenly. He and his now wife were very happy and radiant on this very special day.

Not wanting to put his parents in a bind at work, the young couple decided to wait to go on a honeymoon later in the winter when the diner was slower and a break from cold weather would be greatly appreciated.

The next morning, the newlyweds were back in the diner helping feed and serve the many diners who showered the young couple with well wishes, money, and household wedding gifts. It was a day of much happiness, and both the parents and young married couple would talk about the love shown them for years.

Several years later, the father and mother sat with the young couple to tell them that they would like them to take over the diner, as they would like to retire and see some of our great nation. They had worked out a plan for the young couple to ease into the management and total operations. They also offered to have the young couple buy the business from them, and not to get a bank loan. They would help them in every way possible for four months, and then they would be on their own.

How could they say no to that! They were dumbfounded but very happy. After asking a lot of questions and much conversation, they decided they would follow the family tradition of having a mom-and-pop diner within a community of friends.

The next few months had the young woman shadowing her mother-in-law and learning the baking part of the business. The son showed a strong interest in the business accounting and knew his mom would teach him all he needed to know. He wanted to continue the smoked menu items, and he would be responsible for that. They would hire a line cook for the breakfast and lunch meals, and everything would be just fine.

When the four months were up, the parents set out to discover America in their new RV, and the going-away party for them was heartwarming as the customers all came to show their appreciation and thanks to them for the years they had fed them well and served them with a smile.

One of the things his parents never did was to argue and fight in front of employees or customers. The young man explained how important that was to him. He told his wife, "No matter how mad you are at me or events, please do not air our dirty laundry in public." She agreed that that was not the thing to do, and she would respect his wishes.

As the years went by, they did a few remodel changes, upgrade changes and kept the business pretty much the same as his folks had run. They continued to have a big Saint Patrick's Day feed and a Veterans Day free meal for all military. They continued the Fourth of July BBQ, and of course they closed for Easter and Christmas.

After owning the diner for seventeen years, they had a fire one night that very much scared them. It all turned out all right in the end, but it is a hardship that no business owner wants to deal with.

Smelling smoke that seemed heavier than the meat smoker smoke, the husband got up in the night and realized the back of the kitchen by the bathrooms and with the connecting wall to their home was all on fire. His 9-1-1 call got the fire trucks on-site very quickly, and the damage was all confined to the kitchen, bathroom, and the common wall. It was determined that the fire started from the men's bathroom, where it was more than likely a smoldering cigarette in the trash started it all. The sounds of the fire sirens to this day amplify in their brains.

Not all was lost, and with insurance, they were able to rebuild and remodel the kitchen somewhat with a better design. They expanded his smoker units and built very nice bathrooms. They were out of commission for six months, and it gave the couple the chance for their long-awaited honeymoon, only twenty years late! They went to Seattle and fished the sound. They then went to Alaska and had a wonderful time. The fire was almost like a blessing to them. It allowed them to do something they would have never done.

When they returned and got the diner ready for their grand reopening, they were so happy to be back doing what they loved to do in the almost-brand-new diner.

Everyone came, all the friends and customers who had supported them over the years. They laughed and cried and fed everyone the best homemade thank-you meal. It again was an event that meant the world to them.

So they added one more special day on the calendar, and each year thereafter, they celebrated their fire reopening day. They served special fire house food and of course lots of smoked meats. It was looked forward to by everyone who came on a regular basis to eat.

Many years later, they too decided to retire. Not having children, they had no family tradition to pass the diner on to. They advertised it for sale, and a young couple inquired about it. Having been there once, they worked out a deal very much like the original parents worked for them. They worked with them for six months to teach them all the ins and outs. They also had a huge going-away party with many new faces as their older friends and customers were now gone. It was just as great, and the families of customers were just as thankful for the years they fed and served them with a smile.

Today in the park they talk about their blessed life and how a fire siren sound reminds them of years of working together and serving the best homemade food to the friends they made over the years. They wish the new owners nothing but success and pray they too can start a family tradition that will pass from generation to generation.

Blind Faith

A FEW LEAVES ON THE trees are starting to change. As we get ready to close out the summer months and fall into autumn, I reflect on how beautiful the autumn colors are. Beauty is in the eye of the beholder they say. I love the abundance the fall brings to the table and colors. Others bemoan the passing of summer and the fast-forward into winter. I don't dwell on what is to come next, I want only to enjoy the walk in the oaks, which are magnificent with their height, strength, endurance, and protection they provide.

Sitting on one of the many benches the park has placed all along the walking path is an older couple. He has dark glasses and is hanging on to a cane. They too are enjoying the large old oaks and the experience of being in the park today. I say hello. They both respond with smiles and hellos.

He has been struggling with his eyesight these past few years. He has lost the ability to drive, and that is a personal blow to him, as he was always in charge and the force of stability in their married life. Full blindness is terrifying to him, as he feels the loss of being able to care for himself and his wife.

He was a young college graduate when his best buddy wanted him to meet a girl and go on a blind date with him and his then girlfriend. He was not dating anyone at the time and just knew he was setting himself up for a disaster. His friend said that maybe they could meet the girls at the movie and go have a drink or something to eat afterward. He wasn't doing anything that Friday, so he said he would but only this one time.

When Friday arrived, he showered but did not put on his best clothes. He didn't feel like fixing up too much, as he knew this blind date would be a bust.

His buddy picked him up, and they went to the theater to meet the girls. He already knew his buddy's girl and recognized her right off standing by the upcoming movie poster; beside her was a petite woman in a buttercup-yellow dress and a lovely scarf wrapped around her neck. She was pretty as a picture standing there. He felt like a heel not wearing better clothes. He would look out of place with her as she was dressed so nice and he wearing older frayed clothing. So he summoned up his courage, and they parked the car and walked up to the waiting girls. He was introduced to her and grabbed her hand and gave it a kiss. She was a bit surprised and withdrew her hand quickly. He then stated that he apologized for his attire, as he had misunderstood his buddy and thought they were going on a hayride, not to the movies. His buddy slugged him because he had said no such thing, and he threw his arm around his shoulder for a hug, and they laughed. The young lady said she didn't mind, as he looked fine to her. So with a wink to his buddy, they all four went into the theater to watch an Academy Award–winning movie.

That blind date led to several more Friday night movie dates. They would stop at a diner after the movie for french fries and a soda or pie and coffee.

Every time he went out with her, she was dressed in very pretty dresses with matching scarves around her neck.

Each date had them talking about everything under the sun. They each had degrees to be teachers, and both had similar life goals. He wanted to teach math and be a coach, and she was an English major with the desire to teach elementary children. They enjoyed each other's company and could laugh and joke with each other.

On the fourth date, she told him she had something to show him. He said okay, and she slowly unwrapped her scarf from her neck. She had a port-wine birthmark covering most of the left side of her neck, and it came down on to her collarbone. She had tears in her eyes and said she needed to let him see her birthmark. He took a look and said "what birthmark?" With that, she threw her arms around him and knew then and there that she loved him. He gave her their first kiss and very much enjoyed hugging the woman he would spend the rest of his life with.

They both found employment teaching. They had found their life mates and were married. They set up house and planted a huge garden each year. He spent a lot of hours after school coaching, and she enjoyed going to the games to watch. Win or lose, he was happy doing what he had always wanted to do. She enjoyed teaching and raising their family. None of the children had the birthmark. She still wore scarves most places as it lessened the stares or comments.

He was always thoughtful to her and made her feel good. She enjoyed doing things for him and having him be so appreciative of what they had. They would work the garden together, and he helped her can the produce for the winter. It is a labor of love, and they enjoyed working together.

They had a good laugh about his old clothes over the years, and whenever some clothing item would be on its last legs and needing to be thrown out, she would ask if he wanted to wear it on one last date! They would laugh, and he again would apologize.

One year at Christmas, he asked her what she wanted for Christmas. She said she would love a new bathrobe, as the one she wore daily was needing to be replaced. She really wanted a pretty pastel one, as her red-and-black checkered one was functional but not feminine. She is particular to feminine soft florals and patterns.

It was with much anticipation she opened her gift that year from him. Inside the special box was a brand-new red-and-black checkered bathrobe. She could hardly believe her eyes! She then said, "Oh my, why did you choose this bathrobe?" He smiled and said it just caught my eye as it looked just like her. She shook her head and laughed because that was what she had looked like for five years. Now she knew she had to be more descriptive when she placed a gift request.

They would laugh about this bathrobe gift over the years as he asked each Christmas what she wanted. After thirty-eight years of teaching, they both decided to retire; he for his failing eyesight and her to help her blind date with getting around.

They still enjoy working together in their garden and putting up the produce, especially this time of year when the garden produces an abundance of bounty. With his limited eyesight and his beloved wife with him in the park today, he also is thankful for a hayride he didn't go on and a blind date that proves love is blind and beauty is in the eye of the beholder.

34

Wind Strength

THERE IS ENOUGH WIND IN the air today that a few people have brought kites for the children to fly. It's always a little difficult to get a kite to get up in the air. Winston Churchill said it best with "Kites rise highest against the wind, not with it." One of my most favorite songs is by Bob Seger titled "Against the Wind." I enjoy watching the attempts of the kites to get into flight. So often they nosedive straight back to the ground.

I heard her jogging from behind me and stepped to the side to let her pass. She is a lot younger than me and in good shape. As I say hello, she jogs by with a quick wave but no real eye contact. She doesn't look happy. There is tension in her face.

Life has been tough, and she has struggled most of it. She feels like she cannot get through anything completely before something else happens. When she was young, her father was in a horse-riding accident. A bank gave away while he was on the horse, which caused him to be crushed severely. He had multiple surgeries on his broken spine and lived with constant pain. Her mother did everything to help him as he was never to walk again. One day he was able to end his pain with a gun.

There are more questions asked after a suicide than can ever be answered. The heartache her mother lived with and the loneliness of her growing up without a dad made her a sad person with little happiness.

When she started dating, she always chose the wrong guys. They were charming at first, but all had some character flaw. She had to deal with whatever it was, or leave. She always left. The main thing that she dealt with was that she was never thin enough. Most guys she dated wanted a reed-thin woman who never opened her mouth to speak or eat. She never was able to do either and would eventually give up and leave.

The other issue that always cropped up was fidelity. She was expected to be true and dedicated, the guys, however, had no intention of being faithful. She would feel used and disappointed. After giving a second chance each time, she would be disappointed again, so she would leave. She very often felt that she was running against the wind. It was constant, never relenting, always in her face.

She finally met a guy who was good to her. They had common interests and enjoyed each other's company. She knew he took a few drugs recreationally, but didn't view his habit as a deal breaker. He had a good job and drove a nice car. She didn't feel worried at all when she was dating him. After a period of several months, he suggested they move in together. She felt that it was a positive move and that sharing living quarters would save money. It didn't take long for her to realize that she was duped and he was a total user and loser. He was supposed to pay the rent, and she would buy the groceries and pay utilities. Many months would go by where he wouldn't pay the rent in full because he needed money for his cocaine. When the landlord came knocking, she would have to fork over the full rent. He would constantly hound her to lose weight and would disappear for days. Things went from bad to worse, and she had to leave this hell he had made of her life.

When she figured out a plan to leave, he of course begged her to stay. She knew that the best predictor of future behavior is past behavior, so she had no trust in him, and she left. Being upset at herself for again making a mistake and a wrong choice, she moved in with a girlfriend. Things were pretty normal at first as she had never lived with a woman and her child before. She got asked to babysit a lot for the child, and she didn't mind at all. Over the months, it became obvious that she was being used, and it was not a two-way street. She was being taken advantage of again. She again felt stupid and knew she had to get out of the situation.

She looked for other options and swallowed her pride and asked her mom if she could come home to get on her feet. Her mother helped her get settled and then had a heart-to-heart talk with her one night. The main thing her mom told her was that she was good enough. She didn't need to continue to be taken advantage of. Not everyone is like that. She was just making bad choices. She recommended she talk to a therapist who would help her figure out what she was doing and how she clicked. She agreed that maybe she could use some help and would go talk to someone.

The therapist was helpful to let her know that life was not easy. She would face many challenges. It was how she dealt with these challenges that would make all the difference in the world. It was kind of like "if life deals you lemons, then make lemonade." She gathered many tools of advice from the therapist, and instead of feeling like the wind was always against her, she needed to look at it as the wind beneath her wings. She has a ways to go before she can say she has happiness. Most important to her that she learned is that she needs to trust herself first. She has to require it of herself.

So with the wind in her face and jogging to let herself burn anxiety, she will say to herself that she will run her race again and there will be no wind today.

35

Finding a Hero

THE PARK HAS MAINTENANCE WORKERS who trim and cut the trees. They burn the trees they cut down in a large fire pit in the center of the frozen river during the winter months. This maintenance is ongoing. The workers focus their attention to areas of the park that need the cleaning up of the deadfall and dying trees.

I come up behind a woman who is slowly walking the path. She is watching the children play in the playground area of the park. The children are all running from swings to the jungle gym to climbing bars to tilt a ride. They are full of glee. Boys dressed in superhero clothes and girls in princess dresses all play, pretending to save the world or to be saved by a prince in shining honor. She is remembering her childhood and is sad for her youth now lost.

I say hello, and she smiles and says hi. I walk past as she continues to watch the children and the memories they bring her.

She was a chubby child and has been heavy all her life. As a little girl, she would have special tea parties with her grandmother and all her dolls and stuffed animals. She loved dressing up, and her grandma would wear big funny hats and bring the cookies. She and Grandma would have so much fun and would eat all the cookies. In later years, she would have the tea parties by herself as no friends ever came. Girls from school were invited, but she always ended up with her dolls and stuffed animals, and she ate all the cookies herself.

She had a great imagination and would play by herself as her mother worked long hours in her bakery. She would pretend to be a princess held hostage by a terrible dragon and in need of saving. She would pretend to be an heiress kidnapped by pirates and courted off to another world. She would fall in love with one of her captors. Or she would be a fairy angel who fell off her cloud and needed to be saved by a male pixie as she couldn't yet fly. She had hours of fun pretending in her room as she didn't go outside to play much. The other children didn't play with her much as she couldn't run around fast like them. She was chosen last for all teams and eliminated first. Her mother would comfort her with doughnuts and cream puffs, cakes, pies, and cookies as they talked each evening after her mom closed her shop. She came from a family of bakers.

They were well-known in the community for the beautiful wedding cakes and the tantalizing confections they produced. When she got old enough to help, she spent most all her time in the bakery learning the craft or reading books and eating day-old baked goods. She really didn't have any desire to go out and play. Her life of pleasure was through what she read in stories and what she put in her mouth.

When she got older, she actively learned how to make the specialty baked items. She was quite talented with applying the frosting to cakes and cupcakes. She really enjoyed making the wedding mints, bonbons, and cookies. She could eat as she worked and was very happy in her work. She learned to make the sugar roses for the cakes and ate the mistakes. She painstakingly applied lots of detail to her birthday, wedding, anniversary, and graduation cakes and cupcakes. Her favorite cakes to decorate were the Mother's Day ones. She always thought about her grandma and the fun they had together as a child. She missed her a lot.

When she wasn't working, she spent her time reading self-help books and snacking. She never followed the advice she read about as she felt she didn't have the time. Mostly it was that she didn't have the desire. When she got older and out of school, she would fill her evenings with movies, plays, musicals, and community theater shows. She felt good about dressing up to go out to these events. She would always treat herself after a night out with a stop at a favorite fast-food place for a snack and a dessert. She loved ice cream and ate a quart at a sitting most every time. As she got older, she took on more and more responsibilities with her mom's bakery. Her mom was slowing down, and multiple health problems were plaguing her. When her mother was forced to change her eating habits due to diabetes issues, she was not moved to try and correct any of her eating habits. As happy-go-lucky as she was about her life as she led it, she had no desire to change what she was doing just because her mom had to.

After several years of working with her mother at the bakery and the ever-increasing workload, her mother one day sat down to rest, and as they say, the rest is history. Years of being overweight and medical issues going untreated, she had a stroke. Immediately getting medical attention for her, the young woman was with her mom through the whole journey of the diagnosis, hospitalization, and the ultimate decision to admit her mother to a nursing home. Each and every doctor explained the proper maintenance of our bodies and the lack of that is this result of stroke. The young woman heard them, but didn't apply any of it to herself. Her mother would never recover. She never spoke another word to her daughter.

With the full responsibilities of the bakery on her plate now, she ate to comfort herself. Mostly empty eating, or unconscious eating, she gained even more weight during this time. She prayed daily her mom would recover. With the help of the banker she trusted, she was able to keep the business running, with her now as the head baker and a business manager doing the other end of the business that she was not experienced in.

She daily visited her mother, each time reading stories to her and daily devotions. She read books from her childhood. All the fantasy princess-and-hero stories she loved as a child and dreamed she could really do. Her mom enjoyed listening and would smile with her eyes. She knew her mom was happy to see her as her mom's demeanor would brighten up when she came on her visits.

After a few years, she had things humming with the bakery, but was lonely at home in the evenings. She got a small lapdog to share her time at home, and it became a rewarding blessing to her. Every night when she returned from the nursing home, her little dog was so happy to see her. She talked to him like he was human, and the dog behaved as if he were a real human. His love for her was pure. He didn't care what she did or didn't look like. He just loved the attention she gave him. He would sit patiently as she dressed him up as a pirate, knight, doctor, or biker. She would tell him stories about the character he was dressed up as, and she and he both enjoyed every minute of it.

The dog filled the void of her mom not being at home. She even pulled out her old tea party dishes and set it up as she did as a young girl. The dog looked great in his hat and boa. She had a lot of fun with reliving the tea parties, as her new friend ate his dog cookies with as much delight as she ate her cookies and sipped her tea in conversation.

Feeling slow and tired for months, she was pushed by fellow employees to go to the doctor. They all used her mom's condition to scare her. She felt she was too young and would counter them with I will be okay. In the backwoods of her mind, she knew she was probably in trouble healthwise.

Being forced to do anything was not her style. She didn't like change. The doctor's visit didn't go well for her. *Change* was the key word. The doctor laid the cards on the table and didn't mince his words. He told her that she was a walking time bomb. Having done nothing of maintenance over the years, she had followed the path of her mom and would end up just like her if she didn't reverse directions starting today.

So she made a plan with the doctor. She failed daily to totally stick to it. She prayed that God would help her, and she thanked God every time she lost a pound. Each day she would start anew. Each day she thanked God when she woke up. She reread her self-help books, this time with a different frame of mind, and she got more out of them this time. She applied different reward philosophies to herself and found rewarding ways to treat herself without putting the wrong kind of food in her mouth.

Today in the park she watches the children and thinks how they need to constantly be active and maintain good eating habits to have long quality lives. She wishes she had started earlier, but she thanks God she is on the right path walking toward good health now.

Somehow she found the hero in her. The little girl who needed saving is being saved by the superperson she is—one step at a time, not at lightning speed.

36

Sunshine Fix

IT IS CLOUDY TODAY. THE overhead clouds let no sunshine in to the park. I notice mushrooms growing way up in the trees. I've never seen them before. They seem to be on the east side of the trees and quite far up on the trunks. Since mushrooms grow in dark damp places, they are associated with activity happening behind the scenes and secrets. I think they are a bit mystical, and I continue walking looking for how many more I can find.

Approaching me is a woman, and she says hi as I say hello.

She is a critical care nurse and walks a few laps in the park on her days off. She gets her daily steps in on her job as she is very busy at work most days. She has great satisfaction helping the surgeons. Knowing that her job saves lives is very rewarding. She fills her life with the bonds she has made with fellow health-care specialists and her parents.

She and fellow nurses like to wind down after a very stressful week or day sometimes. Being able to laugh and breathe slowly after being under critical pressure with saving someone's life has great mental health qualities. The most difficult cases for her are the children. She has a personal goal to do absolutely everything to save a child's life. Knowing what her mother suffers with daily in losing her brother, she has a special drive to spare any mother from the inner hell her mom lives with daily.

Her mom and dad have had a long life together, and her father has a little repair shop. He can fix anything. It doesn't matter if it's a vehicle, lawn mower, or a hair dryer, he has the touch. He had always prided himself on bringing back to life some item that most thought was on its last legs. Maybe from her dad is where she got her drive to fix up people. He would spend hours looking for one broken electrical wire in someone's vehicle. He wouldn't stop until he found it. He loved his work as much as she loved hers.

Her mom is a stay-at-home wife. Always did. She raised herself and her brother, and she also very much enjoyed her life.

When her brother was in high school, he lost control of the pickup he was driving and was thrown out when it rolled, and he was killed. There is no greater sorrow than the loss of a child. It goes against the natural grain of things. Her mother's grief is still with her today. Her favorite response when asked how she is doing is "There's no sunshine today as he is gone."

It's awful hard to not be able to say anything to her mom to help her feel better. Her mom's depression has had her taking several medications. Constantly changing the dose or switching to something new. She has never been happy as there is no sunshine as she says. She and her dad have formed a very tight bond, both reaching to each other for strength and being a force to help her mom and his wife.

One day she was visiting with her dad in his shop while he was rewiring a lamp. He finally had it working, and as he turned it off and on, he said to her, "I wish I could fix your mom. But how do you fix a broken heart? I can slowly work on any item and finally get results. It's not that way with your mom. We go to church, and she hears a sermon and God's saving grace, and she's a little better for a day or so. Then the clouds gather again, and there's no sunshine." He told his daughter that it further saddens her mom to think about how she will never see her brother marry or have children. She cries for the grandkids she will never know.

Her father then says, "With her broken heart, sometimes it's hard to know which way to pray. I just can't fix this."

She hugged her dad, and they held each other until they could stop the tears. She then told her dad that as a team, they would always be there for her mother. That maybe they should start celebrating her brother's life instead of mourning his death. Giving thanks for the time they had with him. His death was the last day in his life; he had years of great days before that. They promised each other that this would be their new approach.

They got out old photo albums and special items that were near and dear to her brother. They thumbed through and told stories and laughed at corny pictures and funny events. Her mother sat and listened and smiled a few times. It would be a work in progress, but time would tell if this would help her mom. She was going to pray for thanks for her brother's life and be positive for the life that was.

Today, walking, she will go to her scheduled appointment to donate blood after she finishes her last lap. Donating blood is the life-giving gift a person can do for a person in crisis. It is something she has done since her brother's death. Seeing the results of how beneficial blood donation is, in her line of work, she knows she will do this for as long as she is able. There is happiness in her mind today as she knows she will donate. She knows that blood is the magical elixir that the body needs. She will pray that health and happiness comes to the recipients from her donation and their days will be filled with sunshine.

It may be cloudy today, but sunny days are ahead when you know what to pray for.

37

Higher Ground

AFTER A HEAVY RAIN LAST night, the path has earthworms on it today. Slow and steady they try and work their way out of the water and onto higher ground. It's a slow process, but they will be comfortable in their own world once they escape this water world that revealed them for all to see. I try hard not to step on them as they are so good for the soil.

Approaching me is a young couple pushing a baby stroller. They are chatting away while he nervously rubs two pennies together between his finger and thumb. He has done this all his life. His mother smiles when he does it, as his father did the same thing. It's a bit of a nervous habit, but to him, he just keeps himself busy without thinking about it. I say hello as we pass and they both respond with hellos and smiles.

The little boy child is not his. She and he know the full story, and they choose to be together. Their lives got intertwined many years ago, and their slow steady friendship and common belief to do what is right for the child has bonded them together. He himself was a very young child when he and his mother went to live with his grandparents. His father was killed in a plane crash, and his mother tried to make it on her own, but struggled; and her parents asked her to come home for a little while. The little while turned into all of the boy's young life. He was the boy his grandfather never had. His grandfather only had two girls, and his young grandson put years back into his life. They had a very tight bond, and the young man still does, now that he is grown and raising a child of his own.

When he was nine, his aunt and her son also came to live at the grandparents' house. She, having struggled to raise her son on her own, was asked to come and stay with her parents for a little while also. His aunt had his cousin out of wedlock. The father was a rolling stone who had no plan on being tied down or being responsible for her care and well-being or that of his son. He was in and out of her life until she decided she wasn't going to be used like that. It was hard for her to come back home, but it was necessary. Her little while also turned into the young man's cousin being raised with him. His cousin was three years younger, and they were treated as siblings and had four adults to answer to at any given time.

He got along with his cousin but knew right from the beginning that he was different from him. His cousin was selfish and indifferent to others' feelings or needs. He only cared for himself. His cousin's "I don't care" attitude reflected on just about everything he did.

Their grandmother wouldn't have the younger cousin wash the dishes. He would bang the plates together and would chip the edges. The grandma did not like that at all, so she made him dry the dishes only. He, on the other hand, was gentle with her good plates, and she would praise him for doing such a good job. There were other jobs that he always got to do, because he followed his grandparents' direction for how to do something, and his cousin did not. The young man always made the toast for breakfast as he was watchful and didn't burn it and spread the butter to the edges, of the bread as his grandparents liked. His cousin got to set the table and didn't care what side he put the silverware on. His grandparents made him go back and fix it, almost on a daily basis.

When the boys were young, they did all the things two young boys would do living out in the country. His grandfather would get them up in the morning, and after breakfast and chores, he would kick them outside, saying, "Get yourselves outside and let the wind blow the stink off of you." Then he would laugh and rough up their hair and hold the door open for them to leave. His grandfather felt that boys needed to be raised outdoors and the fresh air was beneficial. The boys would ride their bikes down dirt roads, climb trees, go fishing in the pond, and swim.

The young man even saved his cousin's life one day. His cousin lost his balance on an embankment and tumbled down to the pond's edge. He smacked his head on a rock on the bank and rolled into the water facedown. The young man saw that his cousin was not moving and scrambled down the embankment and pulled him from the water. Once he was on the bank, he did chest compressions until his cousin spit water, coughed, and responded. It was a close call, and the young man was grateful that he was there to help his cousin.

As they got older, they had different interests but still did a lot together. His cousin was more interested in girls and cars. He on the other hand liked both of those things, but was more of a sports and music person. As soon as his cousin got his own car, he was dating. He went through girls like changing his clothes. The young man was more selective and didn't date much. He had a lot of friendships with girls and enjoyed their company, but chose not to date one-on-one or exclusively.

After he graduated and was working at the grain elevator, he didn't hang out with his cousin so much. A few times they would talk, and his cousin would talk about this girl or that girl or this car or that. With fair coming, he was asked if he wanted to attend the Friday night concert with his cousin and his girlfriend. Loving music and the fair experience, he said yes and planned to go.

He planned to meet his cousin by the grandstand entrance. When he saw his cousin coming with a beautiful brunette, he was smitten right away. After being introduced, he very much liked this girl. They stood by each other during the music as his cousin was off and talking to different groups of boys and girls most of the concert. They didn't talk a lot that night as everything about the concert is really loud. The whole time he was with her, he rubbed his pennies together between his finger and thumb. Later, she asked him what he was doing with the pennies, and he said it was a habit of his. She looked at him and said, "A penny for your thoughts." He laughed and said he was thinking he should go home, not wanting to tell her that he thought she was pretty and he couldn't believe she was with his cousin.

So began the summer of the threesome. He started going more and more places with his cousin and her, mostly to be around her as she was easy on the eyes and easy to talk to. Most every time he was with her sitting in the baseball bleachers or across the table from her in a restaurant or bar, he would rub the pennies together. She asked him every time, "A penny for your thoughts?" He liked that she asked, but he couldn't tell her the truth. He always said something about his grandparents, mom, work, or the weather. They had a lot of chances to talk as his cousin was always missing in action. The cousin would be surrounded by girls and wouldn't pay a lot of attention to him and his girlfriend.

Once he asked the girl what she saw in his cousin. She said he was good-looking and had an aloof manner like a James Dean kind of guy. She said he wasn't mean to her like a previous boyfriend, and he had a nice car. Thinking about what she had said, the young man asked her if she loved him. She responded that she didn't know yet. He rubbed the pennies in his fingers faster as he knew he loved her, but he could say nothing.

Toward late fall, he was sitting with her at a football game when she told him she thought she was pregnant. He asked her if his cousin knew, and she replied that they had a big argument earlier that day when she told him. He asked why they argued, and she said that the cousin accused her of getting pregnant on purpose. She denied that it was on purpose. The cousin said that she should not have trapped him like that, as he was too young to get married or be a father. She cried that she had misjudged him, and she knew that her parents would be furious.

He held her and told her he would talk to his cousin and that things would be all right. She shook her head because she didn't believe that it would.

He waited up for his cousin to get home that night. He confronted him with what she had told him. His cousin said it was none of his business and to leave him alone. He said that it is his business, as this affected their family, and by God, he was going to have to do the right thing. His cousin said it was her fault she got pregnant and he didn't want anything to do with it. The young man stated that it was both of their faults, not hers alone. It was a fifty-fifty deal, and he could not blame her 100 percent. The young man grabbed him by the shoulder and said, "When a good man makes a mistake, he does everything to make it right." His cousin said, "The hell I will. I'm not getting tied down by a kid. I have things to do, places to go, and life to live. This is her problem."

With disgust in his thoughts for his cousin, the young man said, "Well, it's obvious the apple didn't fall very far from the tree. You are as pathetic as your dad and disgusting to me. Get yourself out of here because no one in this house will honor your decision not to honor your girlfriend."

With that, he was done with his cousin, their relationship severed. After staying up all night and thinking about every possibility, the young man drove to her house and asked her to talk with him. She agreed, and they sat in his truck and talked for hours. He promised her that he would take the fall for his cousin and take the blame. She cried and said she couldn't let him do that. He told her that if they both worked together for the child's sake foremost, they could make it work if they agreed to be open and honest with each other. He asked her to get married at the justice of the peace, and then they would later tell the families that she was expecting. She said no at first, but then questioned why he would do this. He told her that from the first time he saw her, that he was smitten. He liked her looks and her manner. She couldn't believe her ears! How did this "penny for your thoughts" guy turn into a "penny from heaven" gift? She sobbed, and he held her.

She agreed to the plan but felt that the truth should be told to the parents after some time passed, and they were comfortable telling them. He agreed that the truth was crucial, only delayed a bit. He made the arrangements, and they married at the justice of the peace the following Saturday.

His grandparents welcomed the newlyweds to live at their home for a little while. Of course, it turned into a longer while, once the pregnancy was revealed.

His cousin took off, not giving a care for his mother's or grandparents' feelings. He had places to go and things to do. He was a rolling stone, and those stones don't gather moss.

The young newlyweds spent the pregnancy in an easy, slow relationship, not wanting to rush anything, with the baby as their first priority. They wanted to be comfortable with their emotions and thoughts and asked the Lord's guidance with any issue that presented itself. Much to the delight of his grandparents and his mother and aunt, they welcomed their son in late spring.

Everyone was told the truth, and the cousin's mother was devastated that her son had turned out exactly like his father. She bonded with the young woman, and their relationship flourished as she was really the natural grandmother. However, the young man's mother was just as thrilled, and the two sisters had a grandbaby in common to share.

As the young couple walks today and he rubs his pennies out of habit, his penny from heaven is his wife, with the one thought that they are two of a kind and two cents are better than one. This child will always know love from them both as his now father took the higher ground and took care of a situation not of his choosing, but as a good man would do to make it right.

As with the earthworms with their slow attempts to move on to higher ground, the young man knows of struggling and believes that good guys don't always finish last.

Worth Saving

THE CHANGING COLOR IN THE leaves makes a person start to think of the change that is coming and how we must think and prepare for its coming. Hope is the ability to hear the music of the future. Faith is the courage to dance to it today. The falling leaves dance on the path as little gusts of air twirl them around. I enjoy walking in the fall.

I am approached by a man who is missing the lower part of his arm from the elbow down. I say hello, and he says, "Top of the morning to you." I say thank-you as we pass by.

He is on a changing road of recovery. Not so much physical as it is mental and emotional. His recovery from his missing limb took place many years ago. He has only recently found a way to change his thinking, thanks to the loving care and concern of his wonderful wise uncle.

When he was a little boy, he spent hours, days, and weeks at different times with his grandparents and uncle. His uncle was a giant of a man, he thought, when he was a child. He was covered from head to toe with hair. He was a walking, talking teddy bear. He and his two sisters would pretend to sneak up on him as he dozed in a lounge chair and pull the hair on his arms or legs depending if he was wearing shorts or not. His uncle, in his booming deep voice, would growl and pretend he was going to get them. He would then lie back down, and they would sneak up on him again. Sometimes he would give chase and catch the kids and tickle them until they couldn't take it anymore. Their uncle was a kid at heart and played with them. The uncle would lift the kids up high and let them pick apples in the tree that he sat under in the lounge chair. They loved washing the apples off with the hose or rubbing it on their pants before they took a big bite out of it.

His uncle and he would build model planes and cars, pains-takingly gluing the tiny pieces and holding them in place until they dried. After all the work was done to build them, they would then take special care to paint them. Each plane or car would end up being a trophy to the young man. He loved every time he finished one so he could display it in the trophy case he had in his room. His uncle helped him learn to fix cars. He was always under the hood of his Chevelle or his grandfather's Studebaker. He would climb up on the fender, and his uncle would name every part and tool to him while he tightened or replaced something to allow the cars to run better.

His love of fixing cars was a calling he had. He worked as a mechanic for a while before he joined the service and went to war. When he first got injured and lost his lower arm, he spent a lot of days sitting and not feeling like doing anything or seeing anyone. His uncle was one of the first to come see him, and his loud burly way made him cheer up and become a little hopeful. His uncle would sit down and talk to him about things he had never heard before.

One day, his uncle, not wanting him to keep feeling sorry for himself, asked him what was going on with him that he wasn't happy to be alive. The nephew said that when he joined the service, he felt like he was doing the right thing. He never dreamed he would come home less a man. He didn't know what he had until it was gone. Without his lower arm and hand, he felt useless.

His uncle told him it was a real shame that he had lost his senses too! He asked what he meant, and the uncle said, "You can see, hear, taste, feel, smell, and touch. By the grace of God, you're alive. For all your whining, you'd think you'd lost everything."

He then said that he should be glad to be alive because he got a second chance. The nephew said he felt no good. The uncle then said, "Yes, you're no good." With a hearty booming voice, he added, "Hell, you're great! You're special to me, and I want you to get on with it. Live each day like there is no tomorrow." He said he didn't know what was in store for him, but he was there to help him find a new direction.

The uncle then told him that he also had been shot when he was a young man. It was an accident that had happened very long ago. He had been hunting with friends for rabbits and had returned home in the early evening as he had a date to go on that evening. Rather than put his rifle in the case and put it away as he was supposed to do, he threw it on the bed. The bedspread was a lacey, embroidered one. After he showered and was getting dressed, he said he reached for the rifle to pull it off the bed, and the lace caught the trigger; and as he pulled it to him, the gun went off. He said the bullet hit him in the lower abdomen. The next thing he remembered was waking up in a hospital room with his parents and a doctor at his bedside. The fogginess of his brain was starting to clear, and they asked him if he could tell them what happened. The parents said they found him in a pool of blood after they heard the shot. He told them that the lace must have snagged the trigger as he pulled the gun. The doctor told him that he was very lucky. He had lost a kidney and had liver damage. His first response was to thank the doctor for saving him. The doctor then told him he would have some time to recover, then he would be good as new. Knowing that a person could live well with one kidney and that the liver can heal and regrow, he did indeed feel lucky.

A few days later, his pastor came to visit him. As he talked to the pastor, he was so humbled he had been saved. The pastor told him, "You're worth saving, so live. Live your life every day rejoicing in life. You feel you have been saved, and you will be saved again. A second chance. So live until the day comes that his saving grace takes you home. For now, you rejoice and get on with life."

After telling the nephew this, the uncle said that he never talked about the gunshot. He didn't dwell on the accident. He had to live and enjoy the fact that he was alive. He was saved. Just like his nephew.

His uncle continued to visit him, and his happiness and lust for life was not what he was feeling inside. He was angry. He felt unhappy, and when his uncle came, he felt guilty. Several years passed, and he didn't do much of anything. He withdrew from social things and mostly stayed by himself.

Recently his uncle came to visit. After visiting a short while, his uncle asked him what he was doing for a hobby. When he replied "nothing," his uncle said he should start building models again. He shook his head and said, "How am I supposed to do that with only one hand?" His uncle said to use his mouth. He recommended getting long tweezers and holding them in his mouth like a second pair of hands. The nephew didn't believe it would work, and he wasn't going to try. A few days later, the uncle came back. He had model kits, tweezers, paintbrushes, and paint. When he set it all on the table, the nephew said he had wasted his money and he wasn't going to do it. The uncle then got real serious, which he never did. He looked the nephew in the eye and said, "No one is born with anger. When you die, the soul is freed of it. You are angry, and you do not need to be. Your anger is either out of hurt, fear, or frustration. I think you are angry out of frustration. I will help you work through this. Let me help you find happiness again."

The nephew said that he just felt useless and no good. His uncle hugged him and said, "Well, you're going to find out that you are good because I know a little boy who had a passion for building models. Just as you learned then, you're going to teach yourself to do it a different way. We will go in a new direction. We will have faith today we can accomplish putting a model together and hope that it will be a life-changing hobby for you."

With that, they both put long-handled tweezers in their mouths and practiced opening and closing them. They then practiced picking things up and putting things down. They continued for weeks with learning a new way, until the day came when they had actually made a model. It was a trophy, a little rough around the edges, but a trophy nonetheless.

Today in the park as he walks and enjoys the start of the changing of the season, he knows he also started something new. His uncle's friendship is like a sheltering tree. A happiness for him to live and enjoy his life with the second chance he was given because he is worth saving.

39

Harvest Angel

THE ACORNS ARE FALLING. WITH fall in full glory, the harvest for the squirrels has begun. The squirrels must be overjoyed to harvest this windfall. I try hard to kick the nuts off the walking path as I walk. I figure every nut not crushed under someone's foot is one more for the squirrel's bounty. Watching the squirrels is very amusing and entertaining.

Up ahead of me are a father, mother, and a golden-blond year-and-a-half-old child. The little girl is delighted by the squirrels and shrills in delight as the squirrels scamper around in search of the acorns. The father and child laugh with the fun of it all. I approach and say hello. The couple says hi, and the little girl waves with both hands when coaxed to say hi. I had a golden-haired child like her, and she reminds me of a long time ago when I was young and had a one-and-a-half-year-old joyful, happy child. I move on.

The young man has been blessed to be in the park today. He was a little over two years old, and his parents almost lost him due to an unknown allergic reaction that almost ended his life. He was the youngest of five children. His parents had a farm, and they lived out in the country. Their big farmhouse had plenty of room for the large family. He had it made, being the baby, as the older kids would fight over who got to hold him or feed him the bottle. He was a happy child and was always laughing. He had a head of golden shiny hair and was cute as a bunny. He was more like a darling Dennis the Menace. He could crawl faster than a speeding bullet. If his mom put him down in church, within seconds, he was three pews ahead, much to the delight of the church members. He never cried, and he was full of energy. He was as cute as a baby puppy, but a handful.

Growing up on a farm is a super great childhood for a little boy. There is always something to explore, learn, or have fun with. Fortunately, he was blessed to have that kind of childhood. There is not a day that goes by that his parents do not remember that by the grace of God, they could have lost their child.

He was almost two and a half and a very busy active child. His mom noticed crumbs on his chin and would wipe his face. Realizing that he looked like he always had crumbs on his chin, she took a closer look and realized they were warts. It was nothing she had ever seen before as there were about ten of them on his chin only. His mom didn't like them and made an appointment with the baby's doctor to have them removed.

When the appointment day came, the day was a beautiful fall harvest day. With weather like a gift, there would be no wasting time as to getting the harvest in. With the other children all riding in grain trucks with uncles and grandparents, the mother took her youngest child for the doctor's appointment. At the clinic, once the doctor looked at the young boy's chart and took his vitals, he explained the procedure to remove the warts. Saying it would be painful and the child would not sit still and that they would bleed a lot, the doctor suggested they knock the child out with a child mixture of sedatives. This way, he could get the job done, and the child would be none the wiser. Once the sedative wore off, the child would wake, and everything would be just fine as long as a Band-Aid remained on the chin until any and all bleeding ceased.

It sounded like a plan to the mom, and there was no indication that anything could possibly go wrong. She just wanted to get back to the farm to help out. There was a harvest crew to feed, and she had the remainder of the meal to finish when she got home.

Everything went well as her child went to sleep in her arms very shortly after his shot. She laid him on the examination table and held on to him while the doctor cut each wart off and bandaged him up. She was told to wait one-half hour in the waiting room after the procedure so the nurse could then check his vitals before they could go home. After a half hour, his vitals were good, but he was still asleep. Reassured that he would be waking up soon, she was told that she could go home but to keep an eye on him.

With that, she carried him out and went home. She laid him on the couch so she could watch him as she finished up the meal preparations to feed the harvest crew a hearty filling afternoon meal. When the crew broke for lunch and all came to break bread, her husband asked about his son and doctor visit. She explained how everything went just fine and that the child would wake up soon and everything would be just fine. As they stood by the couch and gazed down at their youngest child, he looked so peaceful in sleep, and their happiness with him was tenfold.

After the meal and with daylight wasting, the crew headed out. The mom told her husband she would join him as soon as the baby woke and he was fed. It was a half an hour later when she was done with dishes and the meal cleanup that she sat down and tried to stir her son. He moved a little but never opened his eyes and only moved if she jostled him. Concerned that he had not drank a drop of water in what was now three and a half hours, she knew in the deepest corners of her brain and heart something wasn't right. Her lively, ambitious, full-of-life child was not waking up. She called the clinic and told the receptionist the details of who, what, why, and when and was told to bring the baby right in. With panic in her soul, she prayed to God to please help her, and she scooped the child up and put him in her car and headed to the field her husband was working. When she pulled up, her husband sensed something wrong and shut the harvester down. One look at her, and total terror ripped through his heart. He hollered to his dad to take over and to watch the kids as he was headed to the hospital as the baby was not okay. As she held her baby and talked to him and wiped his brow with a cold baby wipe, her husband sped to the clinic. They cried, and they prayed and prayed.

When they got to the clinic, the doctor met him in the hall. He grabbed the child, listened to his heart, and took off running to the ER. The parents running behind him got to the ER to watch an oxygen mask being slapped over the child's face and nurses looking for veins to start a drip and monitor tabs being placed on his chest. The doctor grabbed a phone, dialed up somebody somewhere, and explained what had happened to this child and that the child was comatose with no reflexes of any type. He told them the mixture of sedatives and quantities the baby had been given and what time it was administered. With information given to the doctor, he ordered counteracting drugs to be given to the boy. The parents watched as a beehive of activity surrounded their child, and he lay there not moving. They prayed and prayed.

When the drugs started working and the child's heartbeat and pulse improved to normal levels, they moved him into a private room. Their child had not moved on his own and had not awaken. It was early evening and about eight hours since the start of this hell ride.

Their little golden-haired son was lying in a bed with a monitor, a drip, and was in a white hospital gown with white sheets. He looked just like an angel. He was a beautiful child, and he looked to the mother every bit of the picture of peaceful sleep in heavenly rest. She sobbed in her husband's arms that she didn't want to lose him. She said she was afraid they had. Her husband said, "No, don't talk like that." They needed to believe. As strong as this man was, he was weakened with fear also. They clung to each other.

The mother said, "I've heard that people in comas can hear you. Why don't you go get some of his favorite books, and I will read them to him." She then suggested he bring a few of his toys so when he woke up, he would have something to play with. They needed to check on their other children and the harvest. The mom stayed, and her husband left.

As she sat by his bedside and sang nursery rhymes and children's songs and held his little hand, she kept thinking of the saying from St. Francis de Sales: Make yourself familiar with the angels, and behold them frequently in spirit; for without being seen, they are present with you. She kept her prayers up and asked his guardian angel to stay close.

When her husband returned with the books and farm set he chose to bring, he reassured her that his parents had the other children and the harvest was completed in the fields he was working. He then set up the farm set with the barn doors open and the farmer and animals all placed in the barnyard fence. He positioned the farmer, horse, pig, sheep, bale of hay, and chicken—all in positions that looked good to him. The mom and dad talked about the worry of brain damage as the lack of oxygen would cause that. They wondered if their child would be okay if and when he woke up. They kept praying.

As the dad dozed in the chair and the mom sat bedside reading to her son a children's book, a nurse came in to take vitals. The mom moved over by the dad, and they stood together. It was after midnight, and when the nurse left, they stared at their unmoving child and marveled at how angelic he looked and how sweet a child they had.

As prayers are answered, the most amazing thing happened right before their eyes. What looked like the front of the son's hospital gown being pulled, the boy opened his eyes and sat straight up in bed. He turned to the side, looked down at the floor with the farm setup, and said, "Where's the cow?"

Totally shocked and happier now beyond belief, the parents rushed to embrace and kiss their son. The father, in his hurry to grab the farm and farm animals, had forgotten the cow figurine. Their baby boy was a true farm kid and, within seconds, knew it was missing. The parents knew there was nothing wrong with his brain, and they rejoiced in their happiness.

The parents buzzed the nurses' station to let them know that he had awakened. Everyone on staff came to see him. The child stayed the night for observation. There was happiness in the hospital that night. The sight of him being pulled to a sitting position has never left his parents' memories.

The child grew into a boy and a young man, teenager, adult, husband, and father. He continues to be a farm boy and works with his father, uncles, brothers, and grandfather. Today in the park, the young father is delighted to share God's beautiful fall and the harvest of the acorns by the squirrels with his golden-haired, ever-so-happy daughter. He has much bounty in his life. Every day on the farm is his life work. He loves every season, but the harvest brings great satisfaction for work that's been well done and a life of plenty.

40

Quiet Attraction

ALONG THE WALKING TRAIL TOWARD the back part of the park is a series of storyboards. Each individual frame has a large glass-enclosed panel that displays one blown-up page of a full storybook. As a walker walks, they can read each page of the story as they approach each framed page. If a walker comes from the opposite direction, there is a completely different story to read on the reverse side of the framed page. The stories are geared to the younger generation. The stories are changed several times a year. I have walked with my granddaughter, and she reads the story out loud as we walk from framed board to board. Most of the stories are educational in nature or about nature. It brings another aspect to the park and is enjoyable for many.

Walking toward me and reading the storyboards as they amble along is a couple holding hands and reading silently to themselves as they pause at each board. They have a special bond. It is a quiet love of friends who became lovers. They communicate with a common and deep understanding of each other. They are best friends. They always have been.

I say hello as I pass them. She nods, and he voices hello.

They met as young teenagers when her parents moved to this city and rented an apartment from his parents. The multiunit complex was in a nice area of town. His folks lived in the bottom unit with him and his brother. His dad did all maintenance and repair work, and he and his brother helped their dad. His mother worked with the flower gardens and cleaned all the units once vacated. They had all the units full most of the time. As soon as a unit became vacant, it was quickly rented as the rooms were spacious, and all units had three bedrooms.

When the young man, aged fifteen, saw the young woman for the first time, she was thirteen years old. She was the oldest of three girls. She was in the stairwell, and when he approached and caught her eye, he had the most crazy feeling that he knew her and a lot about her. She stared at his face, and he returned the stare. She was amazing in appearance. Something of a quality he hadn't seen in any other girl. In the cobwebs of his brain, he felt drawn to her for some reason. It was uncanny, but a good kind of uncanny. He said hello, and she kept looking at him. He found himself staring back at her, and she smiled and made a brief nod in response. She waved and continued up the stairs carrying a box she was taking to the apartment. He saw her many more times that day, and he couldn't shake the feeling that she was familiar to him. It was like the girl you dream about, and here she was in the flesh. She had twinkling eyes, and her face was very expressive. There was something about her that he was eager to get to know. As he watched her parents unload boxes of their belongings, he would notice her, staring at him with her twinkling green eyes. She never said anything each time he saw her that first day.

The next day, his mother suggested that he meet the new neighbors. She said that the new family had a daughter about his age and she was a real special girl as far as she could tell. He said he saw her the previous day and that she looked nice. His mom smiled at that and said maybe they could be friends. After a couple of days when the new family was settled, he saw her in the backyard with the two younger girls who looked similar to her. He figured they were sisters, and he approached. The two younger girls were full of giggles and laughter and said hello and asked him his name. He told them and asked the girls their names. All the while, the older girl just smiled and looked at him directly in the face. The younger girls told him their names and introduced the older sister and told him her name.

He nodded to the older girl and asked how she liked moving to this city. The younger girls said they couldn't wait to meet new friends and for school to start. The older sister watched her sisters speak and nodded her head.

Again he felt an uncanny feeling about this girl. She was a quiet sort and kind of mysterious. He was somewhat fascinated by her. There were stories in her eyes. He just felt like he knew her. Kind of a déjà vu. She turned to her sister, and as her hands and fingers worked, her sister said to him, "Our sister wants to know how old you are?"

He was struck by the sound of silence and knew at that moment that she was deaf. That made her all the more interesting to him as he now wanted to know from them how he should communicate with her. The little sisters said that she reads lips. She can understand anything you say as long as she watches your face and lips. The little girls said that she went to school to sign and that the whole family signs. The young man asked how he could know what she is saying if he didn't know how to sign? The girls laughed and said that a paper and pen worked well because she can write like a speeding bullet. He looked at her, and she was smiling. Her face made him smile. He then spoke directly to her and told her that he was fifteen. She nodded and signed to her sisters that she would like to have a pen and paper to make talking to him easier the next time they met. He told her that that would be nice, and he looked forward to talking to her again.

When he turned to leave, the young woman stared at him walking away. She felt that there was something about him that was interesting. She was looking forward to talking to him and getting to know him better.

From that day forward, she always carried a notebook and pen. Each time they would visit, she would sit directly in front of him, face-to-face, and he would speak, and she would write. He found himself talking a lot. She was easy to talk to. She never interrupted and seemed fascinated by his stories. She, on the other hand, loved this different kind of communication, watching his face constantly and beginning to teach him signing. She preferred him to speak as she loved watching his face.

That first summer was a learning experience for them both. They learned a lot about each other. They learned each other's hopes and dreams. She told him her fears. He felt great admiration for her to be a deaf person with so much noise, chatter, and music, which she would never hear. She told him that she lost her hearing as a very young child due to a very high fever. Her parents put her in special schools, which she excelled at. She is in mainstream schools now and gets along real well. She wears a watch to stay on schedule for everything she does. Hearing alarms, bells, and voices giving directions are impossible if she can't read lips. She has a lot to be thankful for and is grateful for her parents and sisters.

She was fascinating to him. He loved her simple beauty and her quiet character. He felt an attachment to her for some unknown reason. Thinking of her made him very happy.

She was able to work with his mother to make a little money. She helped his mom clean apartments, washing walls and cleaning ovens, stoves, and shower stalls. She never complained about anything. His mother liked her a lot.

Time went by fast, and before a wink of an eye, they were in and then out of high school. His parents bought more apartment complexes, and he worked with his dad on all repairs, maintenance, and upkeep. He didn't want to go to college and enjoyed working with his parents. His relationship with them was important to him. His dedication to the young woman had him on his knees one day asking if she would marry him. He was deeply in love with her, and he would be hers faithfully until they would leave this earth. They had a silent bond that they shared with mutual respect and attraction for each other. He still didn't know where it came from, but he knew that he knew her from the first time ever he saw her face.

She couldn't have been happier. She couldn't believe that he would now be her husband as he was her best friend. He was so kind to her. His desire to take care of her, was very appealing to her. She loved watching his face even if he wasn't speaking.

Their wedding was a simple affair. They set up house in one of the ground-level apartments that he helped manage. She continued to help his mother, and they too had a special bond. His mother had not had a daughter, and his now wife had a quiet relaxing way about her that his mom enjoyed. His dad quite liked her and was very impressed when they taught her to play solo and she was able to learn the game quickly and well. The couple was blessed with two children. There were difficulties with a deaf mom and hearing children. The young mother had a sixth sense about her, and the children were never without her close by. She could read faces quickly and always seemed to know what was needed.

Many new products developed for the hearing impaired made life easier for her than when she was a child. Her biggest obstacle was the misconception that just because she was deaf that she was dumb. She taught the children sign language at a very young age.

The couple only had one large argument in their married life. It was a doozy, and both learned that they would not have a relationship of mistrust or discord. She was feeling a bit exhausted when the children were young. Her husband was busy all the time and kept coming home late. The multiple apartment complexes kept him away from her and the children. At the first of the month when the rent was past due, her husband would need to go collect the rent owed. There were some female renters who would make advances toward him in hopes of reducing or paying their rent. He never fell for this and evicted renters for this very reason. Her husband was nice-looking and a very good conversationalist. He told a good story, and men and women enjoyed his company. The young mother knew all of this and wasn't concerned about his faithfulness before. There was a woman who constantly called him to fix things in her apartment. It was not an issue at first, but a pattern started to develop. The husband was being summoned to attend to some item at this woman's apartment most every other evening. When he would come home and was asked what was wrong at the apartment, he would say it was something simple like a loose knob, a sprung door, or a leaky faucet. He said mostly the lady wanted to talk. Knowing that he is quite the talker, his wife understood why he was gone so long.

She did, however, let worry creep in; and from that suspicion and jealousy soon arrived. Convincing herself that he was up to no good, she began to panic. When he arrived, she was mad, scared to lose him, and disappointed. She wrote that she wasn't going to let him treat her this way and she was going to leave. He said she was blowing it all out of proportion and nothing was going on. She wouldn't hear of it as he had been going over there for far too long. She accused him of cheating. He denied it. She said she was leaving and went out the front door. He followed her and caught her shoulder. She spun around and tried to hand him her wedding ring. He wouldn't take it. He said that he had given her that ring out of his faithful love to her, and he wouldn't take it back as he had done nothing wrong. She was mad and crying. She threw the ring. He was surprised to say the least. His back was to the street, and he did not see where it landed. She however watched it hit the street and saw the glint in the moonlight as the ring made contact. He couldn't believe she did it. He went and got a flashlight so they could find it. As he went into the house to get a flashlight, she raced to the spot she thought the ring was and, sure enough, found it nearby and put it in her pocket. He came to search, and they both looked and looked until he said he'd come back tomorrow. It was late, and they needed to get to bed.

In the house, he swore he was faithful and was very sorry she was feeling dishonored. He apologized for making her feel this way and said that from then on, if the woman called, he would have his dad go to her apartment.

The frustration was still with her, and she didn't write anything about finding the ring. The next morning, he went out and searched and searched. He didn't find the ring. She slipped the ring into her coin purse as she figured she wanted him to think some more about helping her and how he is too nice to other women.

He made a big deal about how he hated not seeing her with her ring. She would look away when he started saying how bad he felt that she had thrown the ring away. Every time she looked away, he got a little suspicious that something was up. So he kept pestering her how bad he felt and how her finger looked so bare. He would stare at her, and she would look away.

He figured she had the ring, so he looked for it. He found it and took it.

He kept the "woe is me" act up, and she then got suspicious, so she went to see if the ring was in the coin purse, but it was gone. She went looking for it. She found it in the back corner of his sock drawer, and she took it.

That night she made a nice dinner and wrote him that she felt bad about the ring and she wanted to come clean to him. She said she wanted to make him suffer a bit, so she didn't tell him when she found it. She wrote that it's in her coin purse and she'd go get it. She pretended to be surprised that it was gone. He laughed and said he had figured her out and knew she had found it, so he went looking and found it and he took it. She smiled and wrote that she wasn't a liar, so keeping it secret was hard to do. He said he would go get it, and she followed him into the bedroom. When he opened the sock drawer and searched for the ring, he knew he had been double duped. He laughed and grabbed her and hugged her until she thought her ribs would break. With a long kiss and another squeeze, he asked her to get the ring and put it on. She wrote no, he needed to get on his knees as he did before and propose. She pulled the ring out of her pocket and handed it to him. At her request, he did just that; but this time, he added, "I've always been faithful and will be yours faithfully until we would leave this earth."

Their bond was strong, and they vowed then and there that they would communicate better, he in words spoken, and she in words written.

They raised their children and now have grandchildren. He sometimes thinks she is lucky not to hear the constant noise of the world. However, she feels bad that she never heard her children's voices or the music at church. He feels bad that she has never heard his voice, her babies laugh, or the songbirds in the morning. She feels lucky that her sense of smell and touch are much sharper. The way he feels and smells are her greatest pleasures as she loves him so very dearly. They walk today reading the storyboards. They have made their own story—a comfortable life story while making it together with the sound of silence.

About the Author

SHEILA KOVACH LIVES IN CORA, Wyoming, and part-time in Minot, North Dakota. She has been married to Jere Kovach for thirty-eight years and raised a family of six children.

She felt motivated to write this book after retiring, as she had stories to tell. Her positive attitude and sense of humor have helped her through some life experiences that she drew upon to write many of these stories. She is an avid reader and has a love for growing houseplants and for cooking. Her strong faith and love for helping others is her driving force, and her wish is that the reader of these stories will enjoy them, as much as she enjoyed writing them.

CPSIA information can be obtained
at www.ICGtesting.com
Printed in the USA
FFOW02n1833230518
46855384-49070FF

9 781641 913324